THE
FOUR
CORNERS
OF PALERMO

THE FOUR CORNERS OF PALERMO

Giuseppe Di Piazza

Translated from the Italian
by Antony Shugaar

OTHER PRESS
NEW YORK

Production Editor: Yvonne E. Cárdenas
Text Designer: Julie Fry
This book was set in Knockout and Weiss

10 9 8 7 6 5 4 3 2 1

Library of Congress Cataloging-in-Publication Data
Di Piazza, Giuseppe, author.
  [Quattro Canti Di Palermo. English]
  The Four Corners of Palermo / Giuseppe Di Piazza ;
translated by Antony Shugaar.
     pages cm
  ISBN 978-1-59051-665-2 (paperback) — ISBN
978-1-59051-666-9 (e-book) 1. Criminals—
Italy—Fiction. 2. Mafia—Italy—Fiction. 3. Palermo (Italy)—
Fiction.   I. Shugaar, Antony, translator. II. Title.
  PQ4904.I21666Q3813 2014
  853'.92—dc23
                                        2013050577

To Roberta, Luigi, Carlo, and Giorgio

I shall relate it now, with the accidents of time
and place that brought about its revelation.

—JORGE LUIS BORGES

What is not in the open street is false,
derived, that is to say, literature.

—HENRY MILLER

MARINELLO

A Western

The first time I heard his name I assumed it must have been a misprint, one of those typos that officials in the city registry are liable to commit now and then, thoughtlessly meddling with the fate of human beings. Such as Condoleezza Rice, whose father, an opera lover, had intended to call her Condolcezza Rice. An "e" instead of a "c." A detail that deprived that little girl of dolcezza—sweetness, gentleness—and instead condemned hundreds of thousands of people to brutal deaths fifty years later.

His case was quite different: he was named Marinello on purpose. A lovely name really, playful, indulgent, a name that might look like a mistake, given it's so often a woman's name. But it was actually chosen quite intentionally, by a father who dreamed of an unconventional future for his baby, a child with curly dark hair and eyes as black as pitch.

The father got his wish.

As Marinello grew up, he became an armed robber, but not a professional killer like all his cousins, his uncles, and his brothers-in-law. It was a decision he'd made for himself: "I'm not going to kill." A decision that changed the lives of several people in that long-ago summer of 1982, some of whom survived, while others did not.

1

The policeman had just come off his night shift. He worked in the squad car division, but he actually was a member of a secret team, called the Squadra Catturandi. Mafioso hunters. Our relationship was somewhere on the border between acquaintance and friendship. It wouldn't take much to push it back onto the neutral terrain of mere acquaintance, or to release it into flight in the skies of true friendship. He'd called and asked me to meet him at the café across from police headquarters. His name was Salvo; he was twenty-three, the same age as me. Too young to be talking about death, autopsies, and torture. And yet.

"Do you know the Spataro family?"

The winningest family of all the victors in that bloody year of 1982. A venerable old-school Mafia clan that had been quick on its feet, rapidly establishing an alliance with the ferocious newcomers from Corleone. The Spataros, a dynasty that was to Cosa Nostra what the Tudors were to the English throne.

"Tell me all about it, Salvo: What have they done now?"

"We hear there's been a shoot-out within the family."

That wasn't possible; the rules were simple and they always applied: Winners kill losers. Rarely did a loser kill a winner. But it was out of the question for people to shoot each other if they were on the same side, within the same *steccato*.

3

For us reporters working the organized-crime beat, this was gospel, this was the Ten Commandments, this was an underlying principle of everything we knew about the Mafia in the early 1980s.

"Come on, you're pulling my leg."

"No, we found the shells. On Piazza Scaffa, a firefight from hell. One on one. And a *muffuto* told us that it was Spataro against Spataro."

Muffuto was Palermitan dialect for sources, informers, literally "moldy ones," Mafiosi who had "gone bad" or, depending on your point of view, "gone good."

"Why do you think they were shooting at each other?"

"We don't know."

"Did you find dead bodies, blood?"

"Faint marks, someone must have been hit. But not much blood."

When I went back to the newspaper, I knew one thing for sure: I was completely confused. I talked it over with the news editor. He told me to look into it, find out what the investigating magistrates had to say. I started doing my legwork, the digging that was destined, as usual in Palermo during the gang wars, to turn up absolutely nothing.

• • • • •

Rosalba was caressing Marinello's forehead.

"Blood of my blood," she said, pressing her lips against his golden skin.

He smiled tenderly at her. That girl was the one good thing, the first good thing in his life, the future in his own two hands, a sprig of hope for a change.

"Rosalba, we're going to get out of here together. We're going to have children, and we'll do it in a place where no one speaks Sicilian."

Then he grimaced.

He was stretched out on a bed in a damp cellar in the outskirts of Palermo. All around them were apartment buildings constructed in violation of the building code, seedy in the morning light, scant surviving patches of orange groves, junked cars. He touched his right leg.

"Totuccio, that son of a *buttana*."

The bullet had hit him in the thigh, one hole where it went in, another where it came out. Given the size of the wound, the gun must have been a .38. Rosalba got a handkerchief and soaked it in water. Wringing it out over his face, she sprinkled cool drops onto his burning cheeks, taut with pain.

"Marinello, if you want, we can call my father. He knows a doctor."

"Forget about it, we'll wait for the Professore. He'll bring the shots."

The girl had dressed the wound, disinfecting it with a pint of denatured alcohol and bandaging it with a couple of rags. The rags were soaked in blood: a .38 is a .38.

"Still, I'm pretty sure I must have hit him, too."

"Don't think about it now, my love. We have to get out of here."

"First I want to kill him. Totuccio is just too *tinto*, too dark, too evil: my uncle is using him as an exterminator. But now I'm going to exterminate him."

He grimaced again. Rosalba embraced him, felt his feverish midsection, the tremor of racing adrenaline. She lay down next to her man and closed her eyes. Her thoughts fluttered away in freedom, as if in self-defense. Before her mind's eye appeared the Castiglioni-Mariotti Latin dictionary: she had no idea why the giant definite article "*IL*" was all uppercase and she couldn't remember what "*apud*" meant. Then she tried to remember the ablative case of "*domus.*" Marinello had fallen asleep. His heartbeat seemed to caress her.

Rosalba Corona had just turned eighteen, and in two months she'd be taking her high school finals. That morning, in the cellar next to her wounded lover, she was facing her first test. The most important one of all. And she knew she hadn't studied hard enough.

She'd met him in a bar at Addaura, the previous summer. She was just a kid, a high school student from the Liceo Garibaldi, the school for Palermo's well-to-do; her straight black hair was pulled back in a ponytail like Ali MacGraw's in that film where everyone in the theater is sobbing at the end. Eyes that made you think of a couple of thousand years of history, Phoenician eyes, elongated, dark, eyelashes black with a natural mascara. She was tall and slender, with sharp young breasts that defied any attempt to conceal them. Her breasts had something to say, and she was doing nothing to keep them from talking.

"My name is Rosalba Corona; I'm seventeen years old. I want to be a teacher," she'd told the young man with dark curly hair and a complexion the color of chestnut honey. He reminded her of Tony Musante, an actor who had been a legend to her mother, only he was taller than Musante.

"I want to teach Italian literature. I like spending time with children."

He'd walked up to the counter and ordered a rum and

Coke. She was already standing there, with her girlfriend Annina, a classmate who was blonde and slightly overweight. Annina's family had a house on the slopes of Monte Pellegrino, just two hundred yards away from that bar overlooking the surf. Both girls were drinking Fantas.

"The two of you, no alcohol, right? You're too *picciridde*, just little kids…" Marinello ventured.

Annina shot him a disgusted look, like a cat presented with a brand of cat food it can't stand.

But Rosalba smiled.

"No, it's just that we prefer Fanta," she lied.

Marinello, deep inside, celebrated this encounter. He arched his spine, feeling the handle of the Beretta .32 touch the muscles in the small of his back. He kept the gun tucked into his belt behind his back, the way undercover policemen do, and he didn't want the two girls to notice.

"No, you really ought to try it: rum. It's sweet, and it makes you grow up right away."

Annina stepped away from the bar with a vague excuse, gesturing toward nothing and noplace in particular, where an alleged "Gaspare" ought to be: she called his name.

"I only try things from boys I know. And I don't know you," said Rosalba.

"Pleasure to meet you; my name is Marinello Spataro, I'm twenty-two. I'd like to become your friend."

She sensed that his dark eyes spoke some undefinable truth, but she couldn't pin down just what truth that might be. His singsong Palermitan accent was clearly from the poorer part of town, but it was elevated by a denim shirt with flap pockets and mother-of-pearl snaps, worn untucked over a pair of white pants.

"My name is Rosalba Corona; I'm seventeen years old. I want to be a teacher."

She said it unhesitatingly, as if staking out her territory: I'm studying, I have a future; I'm not just some chick you might pick up in a bar.

"It's nice to meet you, Rosalba. But don't tell me you want to start teaching tonight?"

She smiled. He took her hand, as if to shake it, but instead he caressed it. He felt the girl's skin as she, instead of looking elsewhere if only to simulate shyness, looked him straight in the eye. Phoenician eyes met pitch-black eyes.

The speakers blared out the voice of Giuni Russo, singing that summer's hit "Un'estate al mare."

Some of the young people around the bar were singing the song and swiveling their hips; a young blonde woman dressed like a Sperlari mint candy was hoping someone would invite her to dance, if only for the sugar rush.

Marinello and Rosalba were deafened by the noise thundering out of their hearts. The kind of thing that happens in romantic fiction, not in crime novels.

She didn't start teaching that night, but three nights later, after thinking it over carefully, she decided that she had fallen head over heels in love with Marinello, as she had already suspected the instant his hand first brushed hers, over a Fanta at the bar.

• • • • •

Everyone lived together. Good people and bad. Victims and killers. Daughters of respectable civil servants and sons of bloodthirsty Mafiosi. A borderline had never been drawn, in Palermo. Before he was murdered, the prefect of Palermo, Carlo Alberto

*Dalla Chiesa, said in one of his very rare interviews that he never
accepted dinner invitations: in Palermo you never know whom
you're shaking hands with. We all went to Mondello, to Addaura.
We all frequented the same bars.*

That summer, a close friend knocked on my door; he was
distraught.

"What happened?"

"I just saw Michele Greco," he replied in a whisper, flopping
onto my sofa.

He'd gone out for a granita in a café on Via Libertà, one of
the best-known cafés in the city. Michele Greco, also known as Il
Papa, "the Pope," a fugitive from the law and the unquestioned
capo of the family that ran Croceverde Giardini and, therefore,
of the Palermo Mafia, was spending his afternoon like any other
retiree, seated at a table in a bar, savoring a pastry and an iced
espresso.

"I ran away terrified." It never even occurred to him to call
the police.

There was promiscuity, mixing freely and with impunity. Very
few were trying to hunt down the mob bosses: in many depart-
ments and agencies of the Italian state, it emerged years later,
Cosa Nostra informants had burrowed deep.

• • • • •

I spent the afternoon at the hall of justice, in search of magistrates who knew me and would be willing to reply to my *buon
giorno* in public. Later, in private, we'd talk about the shoot-
out between two Spataro cousins and what possible motive
might be behind it.

I didn't pick up much information. Around seven I went
back home, to an apartment in a building dating from the turn

of the twentieth century, a place I shared with my best friend, Fabrizio. Sandalwood boiserie paneling on the walls gave it a very Gotham City look and feel. Fabrizio's grandparents had both died there, more than fifty years after building the place, and in the early 1980s, with the apartment unoccupied, the two of us were allowed to live in it. We touched nothing, not the sandalwood, not the Art Nouveau furniture. We added our LPs, our hi-fi systems, our paintings, and the bohemian lifestyles of a couple of guys in their twenties without any clear objectives.

I woke up early every day to go to the newspaper, which had to be put to bed at the printers no later than 1:00 in the afternoon. My alarm clock rang at 6:30, and I usually made it in by 7:15, with a wave and a "good morning" to Saro, the newspaper office's doorman. "Sleepy eyes," he'd say with a smile, twirling his mustache to launch an unmistakable allusion into the air, affectionately: "Sexy eyes, sexy eyes."

Palermo was still enveloped in the gentle warmth of early summer: in a few days, the vise grip of summer heat would tighten. You could die from the heat and the stench of garbage. But in the same city that appeared bent on killing you, you could also live in what seemed like paradise. And it was one of those evenings.

Paradise was what Paolo had promised me: "I'll take you to Mondello for a drink, at the Bar La Torre. There are four girls from northern Italy, just passing through. Each of them prettier than the last. They're here to do a photo shoot, for an ad."

Paolo was one of my closest and most valued friends. He studied philosophy without much drive, but he did distinguish himself for his remarkable speculative abilities: he was the first in Palermo to explore successfully what he called the "phenomenology of windsurfing." With an appendix that he planned to present as his supplemental thesis: *On Windsurfing: A Theoretical Introduction to the Metaphysics of Pick-Up Artistry.* We had a date for ten that night at the Hotel La Torre—back then, as far as I was concerned, one of the finest hotels on earth. A hundred or so rooms on the point of the Gulf of Mondello, with the surf crashing beneath every single window. Mount Pellegrino, looming above the beach, is something straight out of a German landscape painting from the late nineteenth century. Seen from there, Palermo is the standard, classical illusion that, over the centuries, fooled thousands of travelers who passed through on the Grand Tour. A place of exemplary beauty. "Exemplary": an adjective used, in obituaries, to describe fathers and husbands guilty of countless faults and sins.

At ten o'clock, I parked my Vespa 125 GTR in front of the hotel. Paolo was already at the bar, surrounded by the four girls. There was also a tall guy, introduced as the photographer who was doing the advertising shoot. A guy who was too tall for any of us to know what was flickering inside his eyes. No one born in Sicily was tall enough to exchange a glance with him on a horizontal plane.

The girls were called Marta, Francesca, Benedicta, and Filomena: they all looked out of place in a city that had nothing of the advertising photo studio about it. We talked, we drank. The photographer left early, taking Benedicta with him—she looked like Queen Soraya of Iran, only younger, and was as eager to leave as he was to take her.

The five of us remained at the bar with a bottle of Passito di Pantelleria. The topics of conversation: love, the future, our hopes and dreams. Marta wanted to marry a soccer star. Filomena was engaged to be married to a textiles entrepreneur, and in fact the photographer was working on an advertising campaign for her fiancé's company. Francesca had nothing to say. She nursed her *passito* as if she wanted to make that glass last for a couple of years. Every time she set her glass down, our eyes met, in part because I wasn't looking at anything but her eyes. Limpid, as green as a piece of Martorana marzipan fruit.

"What about you, Francesca?"

"What do you mean, what about me?"

"Are you in love with someone?"

"I don't like to talk about my private life."

"Did you know that 'private' means something that's missing, something of which you've been deprived? For instance: that person has been *deprived* of his liberty. That nation has been *deprived* of the right to a democratic ballot..."

She smiled.

"I haven't been *deprived* of anything. I have a boyfriend, in Milan. He's a lawyer. I read a book once where it said that lawyers use words as weapons. It made me think."

"What about us journalists, in your opinion? How do we use words?"

"As traps. You talk, you choose your words. Then other people believe them."

"How old are you?"

"Twenty-one."

"What do you want to be when you grow up?"

"Anything but a lawyer," she said with a smile. She was charming.

"How many days are you staying?"

"We have a flight tomorrow afternoon."

I forgot about my day at the hall of justice, and to make up for it I resented the injustice of her departure. We left, exchanging phone numbers.

By one o'clock I was back home. There was an orange tabby cat who lived with me and Fabrizio. It was a male cat named Cicova. He came toward me with his tail held high: Cicova was hungry. It didn't take much to make him happy.

Before going to bed I reviewed the day's activities. I'd met Francesca, I'd been told about an unlikely shoot-out between two Mafiosi in the same clan, and I'd found out nothing specific, except for one fact with which I was already very familiar: all Milan phone numbers start with 02.

• • • • •

Marinello had woken up; the lowered roller blinds made it impossible for him to guess what time of day it was.

"My love, is it already afternoon?"

Rosalba was sitting in the chair next to the bed. She touched his forehead. The shot that the Professore had given him had worked: his brow was cool. The dressing on his leg was stained red; the wound was draining.

"It's six o'clock. The Professore helped you to get some sleep. He says it isn't serious; we can get out of here whenever you want. After all, I'll be doing the driving."

Marinello closed his eyes and thought back to the moment when he had felt the bullet tear into his thigh. Totuccio was about fifty feet away; they'd fired at each other, unloading two clips, missing each other entirely. The fury of finally lashing out against someone. Their aim was off, but then: a direct hit. A lead projectile had lacerated everything in its way: blood vessels, muscles, nerves, connective tissues, veins, arteries. Everything torn to shreds, in an area no bigger than a hundred-lire coin; but painful, as if each of these lire were billions. A bullet in the thigh: nothing for a guy like him, but it was everything for a nephew fleeing a Mafia family with only one thing in mind—to escape with the right girl, a girl who was different from all the rest, to a place where no one knew how to speak Sicilian dialect.

"I'm no killer."

He'd thought of Rosalba, hidden in the car.

And he saw his cousin Totuccio coming toward him to finish him off.

• • • • •

At first, it could have been a Western. Open with a shot of cowboys, two gunmen face-to-face, fifty feet apart: crosscutting. Classic images, cut off at the knee to focus on the holsters and the six-shooters. Their Sonoran desert was Piazza Scaffa at three in the morning. In 1860, two hundred yards to the west, Garibaldi's soldiers, his *picciotti*, had beaten Franceschiello's troops on the Ponte dell'Ammiraglio. That night in 1982, two very different *picciotti* were facing off, one on one, over an issue of honor and respect. Something much weightier than a mere question of national unity.

Totuccio Spataro, twenty-five years old, also known as Peduzzo, the number-one killer of the Ciaculli Mafia clan, showed up first. His moniker refered to his tiny feet, size 39, the kind of feet you'd expect of a soccer playmaker such as Francesco Totti, not of a professional killer. When Mother Nature created Peduzzo, she skimped on his footprints and his empathy for his fellow man. Totuccio had built a reputation by mercilessly slaughtering anyone he was sent out against. He never wanted details: just first and last names, and some indication of how spectacular a murder his bosses were looking for; the way a killing was carried out was the teachable moment, so to speak.

Killing someone from a moving motorcycle means showing respect for your target: it means they're someone hard to reach and to hit, like the greater amberjack, which is a carnivorous fish. *"Incaprettare"* a victim, hog-tying someone so he chokes himself to death, is a very different message: a sign of absolute contempt for a body reduced to a self-strangling mass; even worse, you can arrange for the victim to be found gift-wrapped in this contemptuous manner in a car trunk, left out in the hot sun of a Palermo summer.

Totuccio Spataro knew how to impart both death and lessons with equal efficacy. And he was unbeatable. At least until that night on Piazza Scaffa, when he found himself face-to-face with his only cousin who, unbelievably, had chosen not to become a professional killer. That was an act of betrayal: turning his back on the family business.

Totuccio looked around, wary of the possibility that someone might be hiding. He mechanically brushed back his bangs; he had a head of brown hair atop a face that seemed designed to be easily forgotten. He wasn't tall, and on his feet he wore a pair of counterfeit Fila running shoes, in a boy's size. He dressed in a nondescript fashion, with a special fondness for jean jackets, under which he customarily carried a snub-nosed Smith & Wesson .38 Special. More or less the way other men carried a pack of Marlboros. But Totuccio didn't smoke, so he always had room for the .38. He carried a holy card of Padre Pio, next to his spare ammunition. For a professional killer, the miraculous hand is sort of like the value-added tax for a handyman or a plumber: it's something that can always be added if the customer wishes.

Once he'd established to his satisfaction that the piazza was empty, he crouched down next to a white Fiat 127 that, under the cheap yellowish lights of Piazza Scaffa, had turned a bilious hue. They had an appointment to meet at 3:00 a.m. To talk. Or to die. Marinello showed up a short while later with Rosalba; they'd taken her parents' baby-blue Ford Fiesta. They parked along the Corso dei Mille, a hundred yards from Piazza Scaffa. They'd backed into the parking space, ready to tear out of there.

"You stay here, my love," Marinello said, laying a hand on her thigh.

She obeyed, and slid over behind the wheel: she'd just been issued her learner's permit, and she wasn't an experienced driver—but putting the car in first gear and hitting the accelerator, sure, that was something she'd learned right away. She'd need to avoid the chaotic line of mini Dumpsters, a postmodern barricade that exuded a horrible stench of garbage, an involuntary and sacrilegious homage to Guttuso's painting *The Battle of Ponte dell'Ammiraglio*. The impetuous charge of a red shirt, the saber brandished by General Garibaldi, the *picciotti* who were dying for an Italy that had never been more remote as far as the populace of Palermo was concerned, a populace that had been crushed during the revolt of 1820, never to rise again. And yet, the red shirts had fought, and they had won.

Marinello knew nothing about all this as he was walking toward the Dumpsters. He knew only that Rosalba would have to be a good driver to avoid them: would have to slalom through, if things turned ugly. If he were killed.

He checked the leather belt that was holding up his jeans. Behind the buckle he'd slipped in a Beretta M9 Parabellum, straight out of an American movie. At the small of his back, the grip of the .32, which was an easier gun to handle, brushed against his spine. He looked down at his shoes: a pair of red suede Adidas, the three white stripes filthy with soil and dust. And then he made up his mind to go meet his own family, a family that was waiting for him somewhere around here, perhaps in ambush behind one of those parked cars.

Totuccio saw Marinello walking toward him. He got to his feet: this was a matter for men standing erect.

"Cousin, you have to be a man. Either you come away with us immediately, you give up that *buttana*, and you do as the family says, or else..."

"Or else what, you piece of shit?"

Now they were about fifty feet apart, face-to-face. They'd grown up together: going to the same parties, the same baptisms, but with different destinies awaiting them.

Marinello wanted his freedom, and he was ready to kill for it.

"Or else what?"

"Or else I'll shoot you here and now. You're blood of my blood, and I'm not going to slit your throat in some ambush. I'm giving you a chance to defend yourself; we're going to fight like men. We'll see who can draw first and fire, but you still have a chance to choose: come with us and we'll take you home."

Neither of the two men had a gun in his hands yet. The yellowish glow of the streetlights illuminated the line of

Dumpsters, two charred automobile carcasses, stacks of fruit crates at the corner of Via Brancaccio and Corso dei Mille, where Piazza Scaffa began. From her seat in the Fiesta, Rosalba could make out the two silhouettes in the distance. The closer of the two was Marinello, farther off was the man who held their lives in the balance.

She saw a first flash of gunfire. Then a second one. In the course of a few moments, there were four flashes, then five. The two dark figures were hardly moving, as if neither one was trying to dodge the bullets. Marinello fell to his knees, and her heart stood still. She could no longer hear a thing; only her eyes were working now, focused on the other man approaching, dragging one leg and reaching around for something behind his back: the second gun. Everything started moving again, at twice normal speed.

He's about to shoot him in the head, he's about to shoot him in the head.

Rosalba moved quickly: she put the Fiesta in gear, gunned it around the barricade of Dumpsters, and then accelerated hard, hurtling straight at the man moving closer to Marinello, forcing him to dive to the cement to keep from being hit by the oncoming car. She slammed on the brakes, got her man into the car, and took off. Heading for a place where, unfortunately, they still spoke Sicilian dialect.

• • • • •

"Ciao? Francesca? Do you remember the other night at the Bar La Torre?"

"I remember you: you're that reporter who uses too many words."

"It's nice to know that my time here on earth has made an impression on someone."

"You didn't waste much time…"

"I wanted to know how things were in Milan."

"That's not true."

"Okay. I wanted to know how lawyers rate in social standing up there in your city."

"Very high."

"Higher than journalists?"

"Are you interested in how I'm doing?"

"Fine, let's start over: *Ciao*, Francesca. I'm the reporter you met the other night in Palermo."

"*Ciao!* How are you doing?"

"Fine, *grazie*. Sorry to bother you, but I was just wondering if you happen to have a lawyer handy? There's a question I'd like to ask him."

She hung up on me.

I felt like a fool. I called her back. She took pity on me.

"Forgive me, it's just that I spent the whole day trying to track down a guy who's half a killer."

"While I was busy with half a casting call for a sleepwear catalog, and I couldn't say which line of work is more dangerous to your health."

She was funny, not just smart: I was already starting to feel inadequate. In any case, she didn't deserve to spend her time with a lawyer. I told her about how I spent my workday as a beat reporter, uselessly trying to track down a case that was, more than anything else, only a ghost of a case.

As we were talking, two of my colleagues were busy tidying up—organizing their notes, putting away their pens.

There are obsessive journalists who can't seem to work unless their desks are clean enough to be an advertisement for furniture polish. One of the two actually kept a bottle of rubbing alcohol in his desk drawer: at the end of the workday he'd spray it over the linoleum of his desktop, and with sheets of the morning edition, he'd wipe it clean. He worked the crime beat, just like me: I always thought that he had a male nurse's approach to the news.

Every now and then Francesca would laugh at my wisecracks about Palermo, the Mafia, life with Cicova and Fabrizio. I thought a friendship was blooming. I couldn't have been more mistaken.

We said goodbye, promising to talk again in the coming days, provided the lawyer was at her side. This time she didn't hang up; she just laughed and told me: "*Ciao*, stupid."

I had just put down the receiver when the phone rang. The quick double ring of a call from the switchboard.

"There's a guy named Salvo who wants to talk to you."

"*Grazie*, put him through…*Ciao*, Salvo, I'm glad to hear your voice."

"I've been calling you for half an hour. The line was busy the whole time."

"It was an important interview; I'm trying to pin something down up north."

"Okay, well, I just wanted to tell you that even though it's seven-thirty in the evening, if you like, I'd be glad to buy you an espresso. At the usual place."

"I'm on my way."

I said a hasty goodnight to my colleagues, hopped on my Vespa, and headed toward police headquarters. The usual bar. Salvo was already there, sitting at a table inside. He was about to start the night shift in a squad car. He actually needed that cup of coffee.

"Are you still interested in that story about what happened on Piazza Scaffa?"

"Damn straight I'm interested."

"We've learned a few things: First of all, the two guys who shot at each other are Marinello and Totuccio Spataro, second cousins. And it seems to have been over a question of family honor."

"In the sense that one of the two of them seems to have fucked the other one's girlfriend?"

"No. In the sense that Marinello went to pick oranges in the wrong fruit orchard."

"He took someone to bed he shouldn't have?"

"Worse: he's dating a civilian. The daughter of a civil servant who works on the aqueduct, a guy by the surname of Corona. Good citizens, and she's a good *picciotta*. But it still goes against the rules. You can only date *picciotte* from your own circles: these are matters of security, and only blood ties are acceptable. They told him so, but he wouldn't listen. It came in one ear, it went out the other."

"So they shot him."

"They shot each other. He and Totuccio, the super-killer. And you know who died? Neither one. Funny story, isn't it?"

I thanked him and did my best to pay for the two espressos, but Salvo shot the barista a murderous glance: "It's a question of territorial rights, big guy."

I went home. I got changed. And I rushed over to Roberto's place: he was a fellow journalist who covered schools and unions; he lived alone in his parents' house. His parents had just moved back to their hometown, a village in the Agrigento province, where they were farming full-time, growing olives and grapes. Roberto, inebriated by the independence and square footage of the place he now lived in, had invited all his friends over to watch Italy versus Cameroon, a crucial match in the elimination rounds of the 1982 World Cup, being held in Spain.

The goalkeeper was a certain N'Kono, who, over the years had become an international legend. On the table, which was covered with a plastic tablecloth, sat several cardboard trays of *sfincione*—Sicily's distinctive pizza, with its scent of tomato and onions—*arancini* rice balls, and a couple of bottles of "black" Pachino wine, a red so dark that the light doesn't show through. The black-and-white television set had been moved to the middle of the room, creating a fairly persuasive bleachers effect: chairs of three different varieties—plastic chairs, baroque-style wooden chairs that belonged to his mother, and wicker chairs that had belonged to his grandmother—were arranged in rows. We cheerfully took our seats. I thought nothing of Marinello, of Totuccio, or even of the guy by the name of Corona. I focused completely on the goalkeeper N'Kono, who I thought was the only new character to emerge that day.

The following morning I called an old classmate from elementary school, an employee of the city administration's personnel office, and asked him if he could discreetly dig up a little background on this guy named Corona who worked on the aqueduct. Just a few hours later he called me back from his home.

"Arcangelo Corona, age fifty-one, born in Palermo, employed by AMAP, the water company. He is the point man for relations with private Sicilian suppliers. You know, with the perennial water shortage, sometimes we find ourselves forced to buy from these people. They charge sky-high prices, but what other choice do we have? Corona bargains hard for the best price, and he turns in an honest day's work. He's married to a woman called Mariapia Cuzzupane, age forty, born in Aliminusa. The daughter of a cattle rancher, respectable family. They live on Viale Piemonte, a good part of town, but I don't have to tell you that. They have one daughter, Rosalba, age eighteen, enrolled at the Liceo Garibaldi. They also tell me that she's a hot babe."

I thanked him and promised that we'd get together for a pizza soon with all our old classmates from the Alberico Gentili elementary school: he was a guy who cared about that kind of thing. Like many Palermitans, he lived stubbornly in the past; the present was nothing more than a deformation, and often a useless one, of what had once been. As proof of the accuracy of this theory, Roberto and my other friends often pointed to the grammar of Sicilian dialect: the only grammatical form of the past tense is the remote past, and there is no future tense. At the very most, if he's really trying to lay it on, a Palermitan might use the present tense.

The theory is true.

• • • • •

The nights of the Spanish World Cup were also nights of police sweeps against the Mafia. The Italian state was doing its best to gather its strength and strike back. Courageous policemen and carabinieri, under the leadership of magistrates and judges who were every bit as courageous, and whose names are cherished in the memory of our country, carried out numerous arrests. A preliminary attack was launched on Cosa Nostra, and Cosa Nostra lashed back with a season of bloodbaths. The first demonstra-tion of sheer Mafia power was unleashed at the behest of Totò Riina's Corleonese clan on June 16, 1982: a massacre of carabin-ieri on the Palermo beltway, with the added objective of rubbing out a rival, the Catania mob boss Alfio Ferlito, who was being transferred from one prison to another. The attack came in the late morning, just as the West German team was finishing its warm-up exercises in preparation for the match against Algeria, scheduled to start at 5:15 that afternoon. I showed up on the site of the slaughter with a television crew, which I ordered to stay back behind the police barriers out of respect for the bodies of the three dead carabinieri.

Then, with a confident step and an irritable expression, I walked past all the barriers that had been set up around the crime scene, until I reached the people reporting to the prefect of police, Carlo Alberto Dalla Chiesa, about the circumstances of the bloodbath. I joined them.

Two cars with the professional killers on board had maneu-vered in close to the Carabinieri squad car that was carrying the mob boss Ferlito. Then all hell broke loose, a hail of lead from several AK-47s. None of the carabinieri had a chance to get off a shot. Dalla Chiesa listened as I nodded along with two other young plainclothes officers: everyone assumed that I was just one more investigator. Then one of the two plainclothesmen furrowed his brow as he looked at me. "Excuse me, but who are you?" I wasn't about to lie: "A reporter." Dalla Chiesa rolled his eyes to the sky above. His men pushed me out of there fast.

• • • • •

Rosalba was stretched out next to Marinello, whose fever had subsided. Their bodies, side by side, were an impregnable island.

"Heart of my hearts, I can feel that you're better already," she said, running her hand slowly over his chest.

He smiled, without the twist of a grimace on his lips.

"The shot got rid of my fever and the stitches don't hurt me anymore. The Professore is a good doctor."

"He left something for us to eat, too: a couple of rice balls and a bottle of Coca-Cola. He said that you'll have to stay in bed for a while longer."

Marinello automatically checked to make sure he had his pistol by his side: he did.

"I need to go home and see my mother and father for half an hour, they haven't heard from me since yesterday."

"You can't use the Ford Fiesta. Totuccio saw it."

"I know; it's put away, downstairs, in the garage. I'll take the bus. I'll be back soon, I swear."

She bent over Marinello, her lips pressed against his: a gentle kiss. He brushed her hair off her forehead, felt its texture, smelled the scent of conditioner. Then his hand slid down, brushing her breast, which rose and fell restlessly under her Fiorucci T-shirt. A cherub printed on cotton that concealed a treasure. And Marinello was with her, with his beloved, on the treasure island. But unlike her, he understood how easy it would be to invade that island and take it by force: the Spataro family had no idea what the word "peace" even meant.

• • • • •

The number 3 bus came by every so often; it stopped at a stretch of sidewalk where, for the past ten years or so, a bent orange pole indicated that this was a bus stop. Rosalba checked to see if she had enough coins to pay for the bus ticket; in her pocket she found two twenty-lire pieces and two ten-lire pieces: sixty lire. It was the afternoon; her father was still at work, and her mother was at home.

A woman carrying a cloth bag full of oranges came up to the crooked bus stop. They waited together. Ten minutes later, the green-and-black silhouette of a Palermo city transit bus drove into view at the end of the street.

It slowed down and stopped by the pole, without opening the doors.

The woman shouted: "Door!" The driver hit the horizontal lever next to the steering wheel, and the rear doors swung open with the sound of someone expelling breath. The ticket vendor, sitting on a tiny bench, tore off two tickets. Fifty lire. *Grazie*, Rosalba said with her eyes.

She went and sat down in the front, on one of the wooden benches. The lady sat down three seats away: they were the only two passengers.

"Young lady, you have sad eyes," the woman said as she clutched her cloth bag in her hands. "Do you want an orange?"

Rosalba looked at her. She would gladly have burst into tears.

"No, signora, *grazie*, it's nothing."

Then, making a supreme effort, she smiled at her sweetly.

In ten minutes the number 3 left the outskirts of Palermo, heading toward the residential districts of the city: the boundaries around Palermo have always been mobile, and closer than they seem. They reached Via Leopardi, then Viale Piemonte. Rosalba got out in front of the bakery where they made the best deep-dish pizza in Palermo.

She lived on the fifth floor. The lobby smelled of chicken broth. The concierge gave her a cheery greeting: "*Addio, Rosalba!*"

A fond, old-fashioned greeting, traditionally accompanied in the street by a tip of the hat.

"*Ciao*, Benedetto," said Rosalba as she stepped into the elevator.

"Mamma, it's me."

"My darling, where on earth have you been?"

Mariapia was a woman who wore an apron when she was at home. She'd never had a job; she'd devoted her life to her husband, the man she'd given herself to when she was just eighteen, and to that daughter who was born to them after they'd been married for a couple of years.

"Sweetheart, you're dead tired. Come here, let me take a look at you."

"I'm going to get washed, Mamma, then I'll tell you all about it."

Her parents knew that Rosalba had been dating Marinello for almost a year, and that he wasn't a boy like the ones who attended the Liceo Garibaldi. He had a powerful car and they went on trips all over the island of Sicily; he wasn't much older than her, it's true, but in their eyes he was already a fully grown man. And all this worried them. They assumed it might hurt her schoolwork, now that she was about to take her final exams.

Rosalba turned on the water in the shower. She felt the warmth spread over her flesh, the slow flow, the low pressure you find on the fifth floor, so typical of Palermo. She felt safe under that spray of water, the baby-blue ceramic tiles all around her, Papà's bathrobe hanging on the wall, next to

Mamma's. The first tear blended with the water that dripped over her face. She tasted the next tears with her tongue, as they began to flow freely. All because of those two bathrobes.

What the hell, Rosalba thought, doing her best to hold in the tears.

The night spent with him, waiting for the meeting.

The gunfire.

The escape with her heart in her mouth.

Marinello shot, the terror that she was about to watch him bleed to death, the Professore, the fever that had finally subsided. His heartbeat like a caress.

She emerged from the bathroom wrapped in her mother's bathrobe. Her hair was up, wrapped in a turban made of a towel. Bare, damp feet.

"My darling, should I give you some flannel slippers?"

"No, Mamma, *grazie*."

Rosalba went into the kitchen and sat down on one of the Formica chairs. Her mother followed her, offering her a glass of water with some Idrolitina, a fizzy powder. Rosalba drank it down in one gulp.

"Where have you been, love of my life? Why didn't you tell us you'd be staying out all night? You took the car, and then what happened?"

"I was with Marinello."

Rosalba's freedom, in the Corona household, had never been questioned. But she was expected to let them know where she was.

"Forgive me, Mamma, I forgot."

"But what did the two of you do?"

"Nothing, we just went around, went to a party."

"Did you bring back the car?"

"No, Marinello needed to use it a little longer. I'll bring it back later."

"You know, I've met this Marinello twice, your father only once. He's a handsome young man, that's true, and I'm sure he loves you, but couldn't you have chosen someone who was more like you? Someone from school?"

"Why?"

"I don't know myself, but they told your *papà* that he's actually a blood relative of the Spataro clan that shows up every once in a while in the papers. Powerful people. I've heard that they're in the Mafia."

Rosalba wanted to find out just what her parents really knew, how far she could push her lies.

"So? What if he really is a blood relative? What does that mean? That he's a Mafioso, too?"

"No, my love. But you know that it's dangerous here in Palermo to have anything to do with certain families. You want to teach someday. How can you hope to do that if you're with a boy who might have a father in prison, or a cousin who's been murdered?"

"Marinello's not a Mafioso. I'm sure of it."

The woman looked at her daughter with love and fear. What did her baby girl know about the Mafia? What could a little girl understand who'd grown up on Viale Piemonte, at the Liceo Garibaldi, on the beach at Mondello, attending parties at Addaura? It was a mystery to her, and she was forty years old. But for Rosalba, an adolescent?

"And anyway, I love him. My classmates are all idiots, but he and I do good things together, and when I'm with him I feel that life is beautiful...but at the same time horrible."

"Horrible how, what are you trying to say?"

"No, nothing."

Rosalba understood that she'd been tossing around adjectives again. She knew it was a bad habit of hers. Natalia, a classmate who had moved to Palermo from Venice, had told her that Sicilians have a defect: they tend to overuse adjectives. It wasn't something she believed, Natalia had explained to her; it was something her mother had said. Her mother was a hard woman, born in Mestre, who rarely if ever hugged her.

"But maybe that's exactly why I like Sicilians: they make even the simplest things warm and interesting," Natalia had added.

Rosalba loved that Venetian beanpole. But she knew that she herself overdid it with her adjectives.

"Mamma, saying that life is horrible doesn't mean a thing. It's just a figure of speech. All I know is that for now I want to stay with Marinello. I'm going to see him now, we have a date. Unless you need it, I'll keep the Ford Fiesta tonight and tomorrow. You have the Fiat 126. You can use that."

Mariapia looked down at the table, and touched the bottle of water and Idrolitina. She moved it an inch to one side, as if she was setting the table. Everything around her was orderly and tidy. She looked her daughter in the eyes: long, deep eyes. So filled with blackness that they scared her.

"All right, my love. If we need to go out, we'll use the Fiat 126. But remember that your finals are coming up, and you have studying to do."

Rosalba got dressed: bell-bottom jeans and a tight yellow tank top.

She embraced her mother: she could sense the smell of home in her hair. She went to the bus stop for the number 3, marked by an orange pole, this one standing straight up, and a bench. And she took the one going back to the out-skirts of town.

• • • • •

"Why is Marinello still alive?"

"He was lucky."

"There's no such thing as luck."

"I swear it. May I be struck dead on the spot. Otherwise..."

"Otherwise you're worth nothing."

"*Patri*, you have to believe me: I'm still the best."

"Don't talk crap: we tell you to go kill that traitor to his family and when you come back you've let him shoot you."

"It was nothing, he just grazed me."

"Sure, but he shot you, all the same. And you, after practi-cally finishing him off, you let a little girl screw you."

"She was coming right at me with her car."

"A fine way for the killer of killers to wind up: hit by a car. You make me laugh, Peduzzo."

Totuccio didn't want to make anyone laugh. Being forced to justify himself in the presence of Don Cosimo Spataro, his father and the *capo di tutti capi* of Palermo, city and province, was not something he deserved. He'd always killed everyone he was sent to kill. He'd never had to explain anything.

Don Cosimo looked at him with expressionless eyes. There wasn't even contempt in his gaze. There was nothing, and that might well be worse.

"Get me the *zammù*, Totuccio."

The super-killer stood up fast, like a Rottweiler obeying an order given in its mother tongue. He went into the kitchen and came back with a glass of cold water and a small bottle of Unico anise.

"*Patri*, how much?"

"Leave it be. I'll take care of it."

The water turned from transparent to milky white with each drop that the don tilted into the glass. The scent permeated the room. They were sitting at the dining room table, and the lace doily at the center was the handiwork of Donna Rosalia Coppola, mother of Totuccio, wife of Don Cosimo, but most important of all, the eldest daughter of Don Tano Coppola, *capo di tutti capi* of both Palermo and its surrounding province; or at least he was until the day his beloved son-in-law Don Cosimo Spataro decided that there should be only one *capo di tutti capi*.

That was one of the first jobs assigned to young Peduzzo: murder his grandfather, that country gentleman who every November 2 gave all his grandchildren, Totuccio included, the weapon of their choice. November 2, in Palermo, is a major traditional holiday. It's a pagan festival, a day of dark candies sold on the street and gifts given to children: toy rifles, air pistols, weapons and nothing but weapons. Rosalia Coppola refused to view her father's corpse: she understood; she showed not the slightest hint of rebellion. A wife she was and a wife she remained. The wife of the new *capo di tutti capi* of Palermo, city and province.

Totuccio looked at the doily and thought about his mother upstairs with his still-unmarried sisters, Carmela and Maria, teaching them the art of embroidery.

"*Patri*, tell me what I have to do."

"What's the name of the *picciotta* that traitor is going out with?"

"Rosalba Corona."

"You know what the problem is: Marinello refuses to kill

and to swear the oath. We can't let a stranger into our home, a girl from a family where no one has been *combinati*, made Mafia. This Corona, what's worse, I hear that he's causing us trouble over our water deals. He's killing us on the price. We've been seeing fewer profits ever since he got the job."

"What can I do?"

"Kill him and his wife: Marinello and that *buttana* of a girl-friend of his will get the message. Right?"

"Right."

Don Cosimo finished his glass of water and *zammù*. He was giving a second chance to that son of his, who really was a good *picciotto*.

"How spectacular should I make it?"

"Not very—after all, the ones who need to understand will understand."

• • • • •

The man who turned the light on was called Tommaso Buscetta. Until the day he started telling us how things worked in the Mafia, we had stumbled through the darkness of ignorance. The first thing that the Boss of Two Worlds explained to Judge Giovanni Falcone was that the word "Mafia" didn't exist: the members referred to it as La Cosa Nostra. The second thing was that the Mafia was run by the Commission, also known as the Cupola. The third thing was that in order to become a Mafioso, you had to swear an oath.

That wasn't all. The first great Mafia pentito, or informer, made it clear that in order to become a Mafioso, that is, "combinato," there are certain absolute prerequisites: you couldn't be a blood relation of anyone who worked for the state; you must lead a moral life, without too many lovers, illegitimate children, or girlfriends on the side; you must display courage, obedience, and criminal valor.

After a short observation period, the future picciotto *was summoned to swear the oath, which consisted of a brief ritual performed in a private home. There he would meet at least three men of honor of the "family" he was about to join. The eldest of those present would utter certain phrases, explaining that Cosa Nostra was founded to do good, to protect the weak. Then, with a thorn from a bitter orange tree, he would draw blood from the candidate Mafioso's finger and let a few drops fall onto a holy card, which would in turn be lit afire. The new Mafioso must complete his oath with the ritual words: "May my flesh burn like this sacred image if I fail to keep faith with my oath."*

Marinello had replied: "No, thanks."

• • • • •

Evening at the newspaper. I was leafing through the sports section of the *Giornale di Sicilia*: the Palermo soccer team had been left behind, in the minor leagues, instead of being promoted to Serie A. I was reading the sports articles as if they were so many obituaries. At seven that evening I had an appointment to talk with a couple of kids from the Liceo Garibaldi who knew Rosalba Corona. Ahead of me lay a half hour of boredom.

Her phone number was scribbled in the top right-hand corner of the calendar, almost as big as my desk, on which I put everything: typewriter, cups of coffee, notepads, pens, cigarettes.

I asked the switchboard to give me an outside long-distance line: 02.

"Is the lawyer in?"

"How are things going in the murder capital, stupid?"

"*Ciao*, Francesca."

"You Palermitans, do you go to the beach or do you just suffer in silence?"

"Sometimes the beach comes to us: last year, the waves came and took two kids off the outer breakwater. Massive waves, full-blown tempest, atmosphere straight out of Melville."

"You're being pointlessly dramatic: I was just talking about swimsuits."

"I go underwater fishing, in scuba gear with a speargun."

"I guess that's just one more way to go on killing."

"Francesca, are you sure the lawyer isn't home? I'm starting to think I'd rather talk to him..."

She laughed. "All right, I have nothing against fishing. It's just that I hate boats. They increase my sense of instability."

"I fish from under the surface of the water. Down there, it's perfectly stable, let me assure you: you're like a floating corpse. The truth is that I love boats, though."

"Too bad for you."

"Fine, let's play a game. If I were to say to you: Francesca, come on, let's go from Vulcano to Lipari and then to Salina, to see the most beautiful water on earth, to feel the gentlest breezes on earth on our faces, to sunbathe in the most beautiful sun on—"

"I don't sunbathe, and I don't like boats. So my answer would be no."

"No, period?"

"No, period."

What I liked about her was her warmth, her ability to shave off sharp angles. I said goodbye to her in the tone of voice of a disappointed skipper of a sailboat watching his guests throw up over the side. Wasted time, wasted beaches. I hadn't even asked her how the pictures from the photo shoot had turned out. Perhaps boredom was better.

I grabbed my Ray-Bans and the keys to my Vespa, and I went to see the two kids from the Liceo Garibaldi.

They were waiting for me outside Bar Crystal, the temple of the *torta Savoia*, the Savoy torte: alternating layers of chocolate cream and sponge cake; a circular tablet of pure pleasure, drenched in a lava flow of chilled cocoa.

The two kids were a couple: her name was Antonia; she was blonde, with brown eyes, dressed in a pair of Lee jeans and a pink tank top. Her boyfriend was named Filippo, and he told me that he was a competitive swimmer: he had a trim, powerful physique, a strong, American jaw, and short hair. I imagined him wearing goggles and a rubber cap: perfect. They had come in their dark-blue Peugeot Boxer. Classmates, in the third year of *liceo*, section III-B. They didn't attend classes with Rosalba, but she and Antonia had been close friends and had socialized until last summer.

"Then this boy showed up, Marinello, and she disappeared: I only saw her at break. *Ciao*, how are you, then *arrivederci*. We stopped going dancing together, she stopped coming to parties. A few of her classmates told me that she was still getting good grades, but that she seemed distracted. She had other things on her mind."

I asked her about Rosalba's family.

"Her *mamma* used to come meet with her teachers every now and then. A very polite lady. My mother told me that Rosalba's *papà* works for the city, or at AMAP...I don't remember which."

Filippo sat in silence. He stretched right in front of me, his pectorals expanding his T-shirt: I was afraid it was about to rip open.

I thanked them, they got back in their Boxer, and they drove off down Via Sciuti. I summed up the situation in my head: Rosalba came from a good family, she'd met a *malacarne*, a bad egg, and her life had changed.

Riding my Vespa back home, where Fabrizio and Cicova were awaiting my return, I thought about Francesca's harshness. That unappealable *no* of hers had taken me by surprise. I believed that life was made up of surrenders, that pleasure wasn't clinging stubbornly by your fingernails to a wall made of certainties, but rather letting yourself slide, with the reckless joy of a child rolling down a sand dune. I was twenty-three years old, and I was looking for higher dunes to throw myself off of.

• • • • •

Marinello was on his feet. He was zipping up his jeans and grimacing. Rosalba was rummaging through her purse in search of something.

"Heart of my heart, you put the keys on the coffee table."

"It's true."

She was beautiful, somehow Asian-looking, thought Marinello. Her yellow tank top was stretched tight over her angular breasts. Her eyes, after that almost sleepless night, had become even more elongated. And her gaze was fierce; the girl who had grown up in the bourgeoisie was learning one of the lessons of this city that was a slaughterhouse writ large: never look down; lowering your eyes is something only victims do.

"I'll go get the car, I'll honk the horn twice, you come out, and we can go."

"Let's go to Ciaculli."

"No, please, don't."

"I want to wait for him and tear him limb from limb."

"You swore you wouldn't kill."

"Yes, I swore it to you. But killing Totuccio isn't murder: it's house cleaning."

"Blood of my life, you can't do it. You're different from them. You have me, we have to go live somewhere far away from here, you don't want other people's deaths on your conscience."

Other people: his family, the death sentence against him. Marinello looked at her with all the love that was permissible in Palermo. He knew that she was right, that taking vengeance would mean accepting a life sentence: an eye for an eye, Mafia for Mafia. No, he was no Mafioso.

He held her to him, caressing her back. His big hand climbed up until it stopped under her ponytail. He exerted a light pressure with his forefinger and thumb on her soft shoulders, which made her close her eyes. The air around them was dense.

"All right, my darling. Let's go away."

• • • • •

In an auto repair shop in Brancaccio, Totuccio was trying to start and stop an Alfetta. The four-cylinder engine made itself heard.

"They're in the Fiat 126. We pull up next to them, while Tano swerves in front of them with the Honda."

Tano nodded yes. He was short, muscular, and he wore a black crewneck T-shirt over a pair of khaki riding trousers.

On his feet he wore a pair of leather sandals. Leaning against the tool counter, two other *picciotti* were spinning the cartridge drums of their Smith & Wesson .357 Magnums.

"We'll do it tomorrow afternoon, around nightfall," said Totuccio. "They go every Thursday to do their shopping at the Standa. He drives, she's in the passenger seat."

Tano nodded: he liked the idea of killing someone who was going grocery shopping.

"But you'd better bring your compact submachine gun with you, the Uzi. You never know. They're certainly not going to shoot back, but if we don't finish them off immediately, the best thing is to spray them with a nice hail of lead."

Tano smiled. He liked the Uzi submachine gun, too: short as a celery stalk, light as a celery stalk, but far more dangerous than a celery stalk.

One of the two *picciotti* broke in. He was wearing a camo T-shirt and he kept his cigarettes under his rolled-up short sleeve.

"Totuccio, you don't have to worry about a thing. Where do you think those two dickheads, those *minchia*, are going to go? They're going to let themselves be killed, docile and obedient."

The two *minchia* in question were Dottor Arcangelo Corona and his wife, Signora Mariapia Cuzzupane Corona. The message had been mailed. Now all they had to do was deliver it.

• • • • •

"Francesca, I've figured you out."

"What?"

"You wish you could live here in Sicily."

"You're crazy."

"No, it's that girls like you break my heart: I understand everything they say and, especially, what they don't say."

"What didn't I say?"

"The most important things."

"Like what?"

"That Milan isn't right for you, that gray isn't really your color, that you'd like to have the sea right before you, but as seen from dry land. We can make that happen. Plus you're looking for someone to get you out of your relationship with that lawyer."

"You're truly out of your mind."

"Listen here: Have you broken the law? Are you wanted on some charge or other? No. So why would you need a lawyer?"

She laughed. A friend, back in high school, told me that if you can get a woman to laugh you're well over halfway there. I never knew how to seduce anyone. It just happened, that was all.

"You need to stop yammering about the lawyer," she said, forcing herself to be serious again.

"Okay. I've made up my mind..."

"You scare me when you say that you've made up your mind."

"I've made up my mind to give you a chance. You and Sicily: eye to eye."

"Meaning?"

"You come stay at my house, a guest for a long weekend. It's summertime. You're not going to tell me that you have to take pictures dressed in nightgowns and pajamas all of July and August, are you?"

"You're crazy, but still, I like the challenge."

I couldn't believe that she was taking it seriously.

"You mean you'll catch a plane and come down here?"

"Maybe I'll do it tomorrow."

"Don't toy with me, Francesca. I'm a romantic young man."

She laughed: to someone like her, the word "romantic" must have sounded like a joke.

"No, I'm deadly serious. A project I've been working on was canceled, so I'm free from tomorrow till Sunday: four days in Palermo. But on one condition."

"Name it."

"That you don't even try to touch me."

"What, are you joking? I wouldn't dream of it."

I'm not sure how much she appreciated the lie.

The next morning at eleven o'clock I was at Punta Raisi airport, waiting for the most beautiful and the toughest girl I'd ever met in my life.

We exchanged a pair of kisses on the cheek, and I picked up her suitcase and loaded it into the back of the orange Renault 4 that I'd asked Fabrizio to lend me. Riding around the coast of the Gulf of Capaci, on one of the most luminous days I've ever seen in my life, we headed for home.

"This is your bedroom; over there on the right is the bathroom. Fabrizio, my best friend, sleeps in the loft, and I sleep in the room down the hall. You want to see it?"

"No, *grazie*."

"You take your time, I have to go over to the newspaper, but I'll be back soon. Today's half a holiday for me. I told them I had visitors from up north."

She smiled, and a spark appeared in her Martorana marzipan-green eyes.

At seven o'clock I was back home. Francesca had wandered around the neighborhood, discovering that *panelle*, or chickpea fritters, are better than *cazzilli*, that is, potato croquettes, and that cannoli filled while you wait are something they invented in Milan, just to make themselves feel important. If a cannolo is good, it's good from morning, when it's first made, till nightfall. And she'd found one that was truly delicious at the Pasticceria Macrì.

She had met Fabrizio, but he'd had to leave early to go meet his girlfriend, and she'd fed Cicova, immediately enslaving him for life. There was something special about Francesca. Damn that Milanese lawyer.

Now she was ready for our first night out on the town of Palermo: white miniskirt, off-white linen shirt, lace-up espadrilles.

The telephone rang.

"Hello, handsome, it's the switchboard speaking: the news editor is trying to get in touch with you."

• • • • •

The Fiat 126 had turned onto Viale Lazio, heading for the Passo di Rigano district, where the largest Standa store in Palermo was located. Thursday afternoon was the best time of the week to go shopping. No crowds, and easy to park in the roundabout out front.

Arcangelo Corona was driving the subcompact, and his wife was in the passenger seat, holding the fishnet shopping bags with woven-cord handles. She had four of them. She was pleased with the practical good sense and frugality that she devoted to her family.

Arcangelo had left the office early, the way he did every Thursday, to take his wife grocery shopping. He thought about what he'd left behind him: not exactly a mess, but still, now he wished he'd made that phone call to the aqueduct of Termini Imerese.

"Oh well, I'll do it tomorrow morning," he murmured.

"What did you say, Arcangelo?"

"No, nothing. I was just thinking aloud."

Mariapia looked at the man sitting next to her: the light-weight gray jacket, the glasses with the black plastic frames, the well-shaped nose, the vertical creases that marked his face. They'd been children together. She saw herself, for an instant, from the outside: a middle-aged woman, unattractive, in a dress made of synthetic fibers, low-heeled shoes, and hair done up in a bun. She loved this man who loved her for who she was, for how she had always been. She forgot that twenty-two years ago Arcangelo had fallen head over heels in love with her for her eyes, elongated like the eyes she'd later give Rosalba, for her intense gaze and the tenderness that she managed to instill in everything she did. A Sicilian woman, kneaded and shaped from living material, with the character of the sea on a summer morning: still and warm.

Mariapia adjusted her skirt, which tended to hike up on the upholstery of the car's seat, and smiled at her husband.

"It's nice to think aloud," she said, tenderly.

Neither of them noticed the Alfetta that had been following them for a couple of minutes now.

At the end of Viale Lazio, where the big thoroughfare merges into the ring road around Palermo, a motorcycle with two men on board, both wearing full-face helmets, pulled out of a cross street and swerved ahead of the Fiat 126.

It all happened in a flash.

The motorcyclist slammed on his brakes; Arcangelo jammed his right foot onto the brake pedal; Mariapia lurched forward out of her seat and dropped her shopping bags, which fell between her feet. A large, dark automobile loomed up instantly beside them. The guy riding shotgun on the motorcycle dismounted with a gun in his hand. A third man got out of the car.

Arcangelo and Mariapia both felt a powerful burning sensation in their hands, their chests, their legs, their heads. Then they felt nothing. Their bodies were now dead meat, bathed in the gushing blood that poured out of the holes punched in them by the .357 Magnums.

A bus driver on a route heading in the opposite direction down Viale Lazio saw the muzzle flashes, heard the racket of gunfire, but decided to continue on his way to the next bus stop. Two other cars didn't even bother to slow down.

Totuccio climbed back aboard the Alfetta. The other killer climbed onto the backseat of the Honda. They peeled out, heading toward the Bellolampo dump: another car and another motorcycle to burn to charred skeletons. Message delivered.

• • • • •

There was a shrill note of alarm in the news editor's voice. His words came across the line like a police siren rising and falling.

"Get going, as fast as you can. Viale Lazio. Double homicide. No other details available. They say it's something big."

With the receiver braced between my shoulder and neck, I looked over at Francesca. She was standing there, in front of me, in a miniskirt that was tearing me apart.

"Right, boss. I'm on my way."

I hung up.

"Francesca, forgive me, something's come up at the office. I ought to go take a look at it; do you mind very much if we swing by on our way to dinner, to check out the story my boss told me about?"

"You already told him you were going. Were you planning to leave me here on my own again?"

She didn't sound angry; her voice was simply flat, matter-of-fact: I was starting to understand that this was just how she talked.

"No, I'd like you to come with me, that way, afterward..."

She didn't let me finish my sentence.

"That way, afterward, nothing. But I'm coming with you. Let's see what your job is like."

In order to climb onto the Vespa behind me, she was forced to hike her already skimpy miniskirt even higher. I silently wished I could be a pedestrian watching us go by.

We headed for Viale Lazio. We didn't have far to go.

Already midway up that broad thoroughfare, flashing blue squad-car lights and a small, tangled column of cars pointed to the scene of the murder. A policeman stopped us.

"I'm from the newspaper."

"Does the *signorina* work for the paper, too?"

"No, she's my fiancée: she's just along for the ride."

Francesca sank a sharp fingernail into my ribs.

"All right, you can go on through."

We got off the Vespa a dozen yards from the Fiat 126. I saw the camera flashes of the forensics team illuminating the scene. Two figures, sprawled back in the seats of the car. Blood everywhere. An official I knew responded to my greeting, with a quick glance at Francesca.

"Nasty story."

"Who are they?" I asked.

"We're still identifying them. We took IDs from his wallet and her handbag. At headquarters they're running down the license plates on the Fiat 126."

I took another five steps or so, and Francesca took my hand.

Seen from the outside, we were a couple admiring not a beautiful sunset, but a couple of corpses.

Francesca turned to look at me, her eyes glistening.

"I've never seen a dead person before," she whispered.

Half the man's face had been blown away by the point-blank pistol fire. The woman was huddled over. A small mass of humanity, red with blood.

"If you prefer, you can just wait for me in the bar across the road, there."

She didn't answer; she just gripped my hand even harder. I didn't insist. Among the cops hard at work I noticed Salvo, my friend from the Squadra Catturandi. I dragged Francesca along with me and went over to him.

"Who are these two? Why a woman, too?"

"I told you. Nasty story, what happened in Piazza Scaffa. These are the girl's parents: Signore and Signora Corona, Arcangelo and Mariapia. Shot down like dogs, just to send a message to Marinello that love isn't everything."

A few days earlier, I'd read a line in a novel and I'd found it annoying. The main character, a detestable woman, said: "Oh my God, love is so overrated." She would have gotten along famously with the Spataro family, I decided.

"*Grazie*, Salvo."

Francesca had let go of my hand. She was standing next to me, stock still. Milan/Palermo, fashion/Mafia, life/death. When she'd landed at Punta Raisi, a few hours earlier, I had hoped there might be a love affair between the two of us, or even just a friendship sealed by a few days of free-and-easy sex. Instead, I had a young woman standing next to me who was being forced to grow up in a single evening, prisoner of a nightmare she could never have imagined in her life up north in Milan.

"I..." She took my hand again.

A police officer almost knocked her over. He was pushing through, making way for the team from the medical examiner's office who had come to remove the corpses.

"I don't know if this is what you could actually call living."

"No, Francesca, it isn't. Not for you. It is for us, we don't have anything else. Go out to have dinner, make a stop on the way to look at a couple of murder victims, sit down in the restaurant, order an *arrosto panato*, laugh over your meal, joke about it, do your best to forget."

She threw her arms around me, in the midst of all those cops, sirens wailing in the distance, stretcher bearers, photographers, television cameras the size of steamer trunks, assistant cameramen with floodlights in one hand, television reporters, and garbage. I felt her heart racing; I kissed her hair. I pulled her away from there, toward my Vespa, telling her it would be better for us to get dinner somewhere in the historic city center, instead of at home. We distributed the weight of death over the array of Norman-Arab beauty that I had promised her. *Beauty is stronger than death*:

Yasunari Kawabata. One of the few deities I recognized at the time.

Francesca left four days later. We made love for the first time the night they murdered the Coronas. Afterward, she wept: her lawyer hadn't prepared her for such a powerful distillate of emotions. In the days that followed, it seemed to me that I'd used a murder to seduce a girl: not an enjoyable sensation.

We said goodbye with a kiss, in the lobby of Punta Raisi Airport. It was 1982. Each of us wanted to leave the other with a trace of love, and a kiss, when it comes to that, is worth more than any other bequest.

I can't remember the names of all the women I slept with in those years, but I do remember how my lips and Frances-ca's lingered, refusing to let each other go, how it felt as if we belonged together as an Alitalia flight attendant, with a pill-box hat on her head and a maxi skirt, was saying: "Boarding passes, please."

• • • • •

Milan, January 2002. Headline: "Drug Smuggling: Sicilian mob boss arrested, fugitive from the law was hiding in Spain." Body text: "Marinello Spataro, 45, member of the Ciaculli clan, was arrested yesterday by Spanish police on charges of international narcotics trafficking. He was taken into custody at the port of Almeria aboard a ship on which he had concealed 50kg of hashish, smuggled out of Morocco. The man admitted his real identity immediately. The Spanish authorities also served him with a warrant for aggravated charges of armed robbery, issued 18 years ago by the Palermo magistracy. According to the Italian police,

Spataro is the only member of the Ciaculli (province of Palermo) family of that name not facing charges of Mafia involvement or murder. Marinello Spataro asked the Spanish investigators to allow him to receive visits in prison from his wife, Rosalba, who lives in Malaga, and his two children, Arcangelo and Mariapia."

I feel a shiver go down my back. One of the collateral effects of memory. I think back to that Fiat 126. To my friend Salvo, later murdered in a Palermo bar by a Corleone death squad of professional killers. To the two kids out front of Bar Crystal who talked to me about Rosalba. And then I think back to me and Francesca, embracing at the airport; love lost in an age of injustice.

I fold up the sheet of paper with the story about Marinello and I call my deputy editor: "Antonio, would you please see that a brief item appears concerning this arrest in Spain; put it in the national news section. Maybe someone will still remember him."

SOPHIE

A Love Story

MILAN, DECEMBER 2010

I'd like to be able to put everything back where it belongs, shut the cabinets and the armoires after placing every memory on the correct shelf. I know I won't be able to do it.

I find a photo of her in my hands; I haven't looked at it since the early eighties. She slipped it out of her portfolio and gave it to me, without telling me when and where it had been taken. I never did find out. Now I can only guess, from certain details, that it was a French fashion shoot from the period. She wears a shirt dress in a soft black-and-white fabric, with a giant houndstooth check, and she's wrapping the skirt around her as if in a gesture of self-protection, her left shoulder higher than her right, her head angled back, almost as if she were a waif, surprised in front of an Yves Saint Laurent boutique, just waiting to be rescued. Her face is enchanting, her eyes wide open, staring into the future, blue-green or perhaps blue-gray, some version of hazel, immense eyes defined by long eyelashes, eloquent eyelashes that tell a story with every glance. Her hair is a coppery blonde, almost red, even though in my memories she is an absolute blonde, a paragon, with her short, wavy hair, of Sandro Veronesi's "blondeness."

Her photograph forces me to go back in time. I think about the twenty-seven years since then, the path that each of us has taken, the disappointments that stubbornly, incessantly, do their best to act as a counterweight to our illusions.

In that long-ago summer of 1983, we lived on illusions. Then I gave her, innocent creature that she was, one of her biggest disappointments, something I'm trying to come to terms with now, and for the first time.

If life were a trial, the story that follows would be a summation uttered by a desperate counsel for the defense.

There's a victim; there's a killer. And there was no justice.

PALERMO, JULY 1983

A spongy object the size of a small apple. It lay there before me, on the asphalt, amid smoking wreckage, rubble, stones. I leaned over and looked closer: it was a heel. Part of a foot, detached and skinned by the explosion. I recognized the structure of the bone. I had a retching urge to vomit. All around me were loud noises, the sirens of the police and Carabinieri squad cars that kept racing up, the irritable movements of men who, faced with an unforeseeable event, had no idea of where to go, what to say. Officers shouting orders that no one obeyed; I could see their mouths open wide but I heard nothing, not the sirens, not the shouts: it was as if someone had hit a mute button. Only video. And in the video I was standing there, motionless, looking down at that heel. I was wearing a pair of faded red jeans and a white shirt, a pair of Adidas amid the detritus covering the road. I looked to my left. Just a few yards away I saw the corpse to which that heel belonged. It lay in disarray on the sidewalk, stained with many colors: the vermillion of blood, the white of plaster, the gray of the metal fragments peppering the flesh. It could have been a young officer on security detail, or it could have been the concierge of the building. The face was unrecognizable; the identity would be established later. There was no reason for haste. Death had taken its time, and we were wandering aimlessly in horror.

It was a late-July morning; they'd set off a car bomb in the center of Palermo to kill an honest magistrate. They'd been successful: along with the judge, three others were killed.

That day was supposed to have been set aside to recover from a hangover. I'd stayed up late the night before at a friend's pool party, in Mondello, celebrating his girlfriend's new college degree. It was hot out on those July nights, a muggy heat that highlighted the shapes of our bodies, making the clothing stick to our muscles, our fat. After dinner we stripped down to our boxer shorts, our panties, our bras, and plunged into the swimming pool in search of the coolness that during the summer in Palermo remains pure theory; basic theory such as material physicists might pursue. The water was lukewarm, the temperature differential was minimal at best, but at least, once we were in the pool, the tropical effect of the muggy air was abolished. We set two bottles of spumante, a bottle of whiskey, another one of vodka—and that one, at least, was frosty cold—on the terra cotta lip of the pool, and our bodies found a way out. There were couples who floated away in the darkness of the water like beach balls, driven by the levity of the alcohol. People brushed against each other, touching each other; there was no illicit kissing, but our hands roamed free, making our time in the pool exciting and, with it, even our friend's new law degree—if you didn't look too close, in the night, she resembled a Sicilian Liz Taylor, young and ready for anything.

I was twenty-four years old, I was a working journalist, and like a naive character out of Flaubert, I believed that everything was still possible. And to some extent, it was.

There were those who left the party at 2:00 a.m., while others lingered on, waiting for who knows what. I was one of the hangers-on: just under the surface of the tepid baby-blue water, I'd withstood the advances of someone else's lusty young wife, while a girl from Rome in her early twenties, whose acquaintance my fingertips had made first, and who closely resembled Barbra Streisand in *What's Up, Doc?*, decided to come home with me, on my oversized gray Vespa scooter, dressed in nothing but a white sheet that on her looked like an evening gown by Fausto Sarli. Her name was Livia; she had elongated eyes and a Streisand nose, of course, a mouth that looked like something out of Man Ray and breasts that helped me to understand the meaning of the word "breasts."

She wrapped her arms around me, clinging to my belly— still flat in those days—as I drove back from Mondello and did my best to remember where I lived. The warm air of the Palermo night dried our hair. There had been so much alcohol, and all we wanted was to survive. Me, her, the Vespa. We'd get around to sex, all in good time, or not at all. Back then, that word didn't conjure up great expectations. We had sex, we dreamed up sex, we rejected sex: every day was an erotic calendar without any preset appointments. All we knew about AIDS was that it was an exotic novelty that appeared in articles datelined from the United States.

"Fabrizio sleeps in there, and this is my bedroom."

Livia allowed herself to be led into the apartment that I shared with my best friend. The guided tour ended on my bed.

That morning I was awakened by a noise louder than my alarm clock, which at 6:30—precisely and mechanically—had performed its assigned task but had then been hushed by my floppy hand, in a complete and irresponsible post-alcohol haze. The noise came from the rotors of a helicopter whose blades were chopping several hundred yards straight over-head. It was a summer of serial massacres, a couple of corpses a day, but police and Carabinieri helicopters rose into the air only when the murder was something "enormous." That morning, something enormous must have happened, and I was in bed, naked, next to a young woman who was making the noises someone makes when they're having a hard time regaining consciousness.

I hopped out of bed and called the newspaper, and the switchboard operator told me about the car bomb.

"It just happened a little while ago. The boss says you need to get down there immediately, that you're an asshole for not being there already...Get moving."

I ran my fingers over Livia's derriere, told her that there was breakfast in the other room, a generic "in the other room" that I indicated somewhere between the hands of a generous fate and those of my good friend Fabrizio, who was in his room, still asleep. I brushed my teeth, put on the red jeans and white shirt I'd been wearing the night before, grabbed my Ray-Bans, the keys to the Vespa, a pack of cig-arettes, and my wallet, and set out on an obstacle course through the paralyzed city of Palermo. A blend of fear and shock, shattered nerves, the after-scent of a dynamite explosion in the air, detectable five hundred yards away from the smoking urban crater.

After spending an hour at the blast site, I went back to the newspaper. The doorman didn't smile; he limited himself to arching his eyebrows: "It was terrible, right?" The day went by in a tangled neurosis: we reporters writing articles about death, laying out horrifying pages, screaming headlines; the newsies shouting in the street, with stacks of papers poised on their left arms: *"Quanti nni murieru!"*—the death count. Evening never seemed to arrive, and those long days did nothing to help us forget or find a place of solace. We were young people, witnesses to a massacre, and we had no way of conveying to the world what was happening before our eyes. Witnesses unable to speak, newspapers printed in blank ink.

• • • • •

For me, the evening came on muggy and dolorous. We went our separate ways, back to a Palermo that, far from the bomb crater, could seem like any seaside city caught in a moment of summertime chaos. Not the slaughterhouse it had become. When I got home, I saw that my answering machine was blinking.

"Buddy, there's a party at Totino's house, out at Vergine Maria. Call me and I'll tell you all about it." It was Paolo. He wasn't working: lots of little clues pointed to that. The message was one of them.

I took a shower at room temperature, one hundred degrees. I put on a pair of dark Wranglers and another white shirt. I found a note from Livia, under the carriage return of my Olivetti Lettera 22: "I had a good time: I like Palermo. *Ciao*. Livia." I folded it and set it on the nightstand. The judge and his bodyguards thought they liked it, too.

I called Paolo back.

"It's me. What is this party?"

"What have you been doing until now?"

"Collecting corpses."

"Well, did you at least wash your hands?"

"Cut it out, I don't feel like going."

"But you ought to: Totino has invited lots of lovely people to come to his *tonnara*."

"Who'll be there?"

He reeled off a list of names I'd never heard before. Then he added: "Ah, Elena's going to be there, too, with a Belgian girlfriend."

Two hours later I was pulling up in Vergine Maria. Night was coming on, signaled by the drop in muggy humidity, the sky over the sea was spangled with stars, and my mood was like that of somebody who'd been heavily drugged.

Totino's *tonnara*—a watery maze just offshore used to catch and slaughter tuna, which can be fourteen feet long and weigh close to a thousand pounds—was one of the few places left from the Palermo of the past, the *Palermo felicissima*, to have survived the ravages of the twentieth century. It was from there, a century ago, that the launches set out for the *mattanza*—the slaughter. The "chamber of death" was devised at the orders of the *rais*, or local headman, off what was now a provincial coastline filled with dives and garbage; in 1880 it had been a fisherman's paradise, just three miles away from a city that had until recently been under Bourbon rule. The *tonnara* had always belonged to Totino's family, the Guardalbene family of Santa Flavia. They were out of money as the second millennium drew to its end, but they had plenty of crumbling properties and a great personal allure. Totino was one of those Sicilian hidalgos who had, at age thirty, done everything except the normal things that thirty-year-olds have done. He'd spent two seasons in Madagascar, where he'd made a living by recovering wrecks from the bottom of the sea; he'd made cocktails in a hotel in West Berlin and he'd started a flourishing florist's shop in New York in 1981. More recently he'd withdrawn to the family home, to the *tonnara*, to explore the relationship between preamplification and amplification. That summer he intended to show us the results of his studies. His garden was blessed with perfect acoustics and sound quality. Totino and I shared a common credo: the music of the eighties wasn't worth listening to. Everything that humanity had to say in terms of rock music had already been said during the previous decade. And so, that night, on the two Thorens turntables, only records by Pink Floyd, Led Zeppelin, King Crimson, Yes, Deep Purple, Emerson Lake & Palmer, and Genesis were welcome: the musical language that allowed us to understand each other at first glance. At first hearing.

I glimpsed the silhouette of Paolo in the garden, where Totino had set up a rudimentary dance floor. I got closer. He was lost in an unlikely slow dance to the tune of "Money," with a short girl, a redhead with a red face and red lips.

"Paolo, I'm here," I broke in, giving her an out. The girl, freed from the embrace, nodded a hello and moved quickly away. I liked her red lips. Paolo was clearly feeling the urge to hit me. But all he said was: "What the fuck?"

"Okay, sorry. How was I supposed to know that you were holding her prisoner?"

Paolo asked me about my day, with the vagueness of someone who lives on a different planet from you and is showing interest in the problems facing your species purely out of courtesy.

"Turn out all right in the end?"

"No, it turned out all wrong. We're destined for extinction," I replied.

"Look, we're at a party, you know. You can't bust my balls like this."

"It's been a terrible day, Paolo. Too much blood. Palermo's going to drown in it."

Paolo took one look at me and understood that I wasn't trying to make myself tormented and interesting in the eyes of women who weren't there, that I wasn't playing the part of a character out of Chandler, that I hadn't stepped out of the screen from *Chinatown* with my nose cut to ribbons. It was as simple as that: we were drowning in blood. He didn't know whose blood. I did.

"Okay, okay, but see if you can stop thinking about it for two hours. Just promise me that." His gaze went past me, and his eyes lit up: "Oh, Elena's here."

She came toward us with a smile on her lips, hand in hand with a slender blonde girl who was taller than her, prettier than her, and that's saying a lot. Elena was twenty years old and she dressed like the sister of everyone we knew, like the girlfriend of everyone we knew: jeans hugging her hips, close-fitting blouses that let you guess at her breasts, or else solid-colored stretchy T-shirts, because we were left-wingers, and as far as we were concerned, pastel colors were strictly for Fascists. For some girls who weren't exactly endowed by nature, that uniform spelled death for any hope of romantic adventures, but for girls like Elena it was quite the other way around. Her southern Italian eyes, full of warmth in every gaze, her low voice, her pitch-black hair, thick and glistening like an Asian woman's, her curves, revealed at every step, and that smile she wore as she approached us, made her—to Paolo, to me, to our group of friends—a catalog of femininity to leaf through at our leisure, the album of all desires and also, amazingly, of friendship. She was easy to be with, but she was very hard to *be with*. Elena was a dancer, she wanted to become an *étoile*, and she'd moved to Belgium to study. But she didn't have the gift, as a pitiless *madame* of Maurice Béjart's school in Brussels had told her during a three-month course she'd taken there. She'd returned home with the bitter taste of her first frustration still in her mouth. She was the daughter of one of the haut bourgeois citizens of Palermo, the daughter of intellectuals, with a brilliant and beautiful mother who was a fine sculptor.

The months she'd spent in Brussels with Béjart had left Elena a legacy: aside from her first bitter aftertaste, she'd made a new friend. One of those friendships that form between shipwrecked survivors, as they cling to the cobbled-together rafts of chance, on the rough swells of growing up; friendships that, if life is generous, can become formative friendships, friendships of passage, friendships for a lifetime. Gifts of fate destined to change us, to make our lives more complete, or, in most cases, experiences of a summer, destined to amount to nothing. That gift with an uncertain future, the night of the *tonnara*, was holding Elena by the hand.

"*Bonjour, je m'appelle Sophie,*" she said in a voice barely louder than a whisper.

It was night, and the speakers were pumping out impressive bass lines, possibly Greg Lake. It occurred to me that when French people are introduced, they say *bonjour* even in the dark.

"This is my friend Sophie, she's French," said Elena.

"*Ciao*, Sophie, my name is Paolo. They told me that you were Belgian."

She had the largest, most expressive eyes I'd ever seen in my life. In the dark, I thought they were a light hazel, or else some color invented especially for her. The proportions of her face emanated a sense of perfection, confirmed by her full, glistening lips, a natural pink, that opened into a smile aimed at Paolo.

"Je ne comprends pas bien l'italien, excusez-moi."

She ran a hand through her short, wavy hair; she turned to look at me, her smile widening as she adjusted her miniskirt with her right hand.

"Enchanté," I said, in agony. Then I added my name.

That girl had immediately taken me to an uncomfortable place, had pushed me into a sense of malaise that, after a day of torment like the one I had just been through, I couldn't tolerate for long. Back then, I had decided that I had only one technique available to me to fight that sense of malaise within myself, and it was unmistakably derived from Zen Buddhism: I would balance my weight, shifting it back and forth, two or three or ten times, from one leg to the other, until the anxiety went away. I did it, imperceptibly. No good. I tried another approach, saying over and over to myself: *she's another girl on another night in Palermo, she's another girl on another night in Palermo.* Again, no good. Sophie held her eyes on me for three seconds, perhaps because her curiosity had been aroused by my courteous phrase. I found her beauty frightening.

"Sophie went to dance school with me in Brussels," Elena explained. "She's from Paris, she's a model, and now she'd like a cigarette."

I handed her a Camel. She took it and thanked me. She tore off the filter and put what was left between her lips.

Paolo and Elena went off to get a gin and tonic, while I stayed behind with Sophie to exchange our first few words. The soundtrack was Pink Floyd—Dave Gilmour's guitar. Behind us was a view of the marina of Vergine Maria, the little wooden launches moored like herringbones, each of them given a name that hearkened back to the Catholic tradition of suffering: Madonna del Dolore, Madre dei Peccati, San Giovanni Decollato—Mother of Pain, Mother of Sins, St. John Beheaded.

"Why are you in Sicily?" I asked her in the best French I could muster.

"This summer I didn't want to do anything, just spend a little time at the beach. Elena told me about her house, her family, the blue of the Aeolian Islands."

"So you're on vacation. Everyone comes here on vacation; I've never met anybody who's come to Sicily for work. Foreigners, forget about it."

"What do you do?"

"I write, and I also present the news on a Sicilian television station. I'm a journalist."

I asked if she wanted something to eat, something to drink, or if she wanted to take a little aimless stroll. She smiled for the second time. She said yes to a glass of wine, which I brought her. She asked for another Camel. Then she suggested wandering toward the boundaries of the garden, where the view of the marina was clearer and all-encompassing. Elena and Paolo were behind us, a few dozen yards.

Sophie had a graceful loveliness that I'd never before encountered in any woman I'd met. Every move she made was the quiet flow of a body on the earth's crust, frictionless, without wasted energy; every gesture corresponded to a small prayer of perfection, of elegance. I watched her walk before me. Following her was the easiest thing on earth.

We came to the parapet. Down below us was the marina with its waterfront and its tiny breakwater. I asked her about Paris, where she lived and with whom, imagining her with an array of spectacularly handsome boyfriends, or else perhaps boyfriends who were skinny, angry, and *maudit*, an assortment of latter-day Pierre Clémentis, unbeatable rivals for people like me, like us—so Mediterranean, so sentimental, so emotional; in any case, boyfriends who were up to her level, who spoke better French than me because, after all, they were French and I wasn't. In other words, I was curious and, at the same time, I didn't want to know. She answered.

"Nineteenth arrondissement, toward the Avenue Jean Jaurès. I live with my mother, just her and me, no papa, no sisters, no brothers. We're a Norman family, we come from Deauville. No, I don't have a special love for horses. My mother is a shop clerk. My father abandoned us both when I was six months old, so *Maman* brought me to Paris. I heard that my father was killed two years ago, in Canada, hit by a truck."

I wanted to ask her how there could be so much beauty in her. Luckily, I realized that it was a really stupid question. Beauty is assigned randomly, assembled like the atoms of primordial elements, and it creates miracles or disasters; or else something average, like most of the world, the common-sense middle, average beauty that is like average ugliness, a non-virtue destined to leave traces of itself only in the memories of those who are closest: wives, husbands, sons, parents. Sophie had been favored by chance, and she abounded in beauty. Beauty is the only virtue, as Oscar Wilde said, that needs no explanation.

• • • • •

There was a sharp contrast between the death around us and the beauty inside us. We were attractive young people, our hair was tousled, we were cheerful, and we were forced to employ our talents in a theater of horror.

Judge Rocco Chinnici was killed on the morning of July 29, 1983. The Corleonese, under the leadership of Totò Riina, filled a Fiat 126 with TNT, using a remote control to set off the explosive the minute the magistrate walked out the front door of his apartment building, with his police security detail. A Lebanese informant, a narcotics trafficker, had called police headquarters a few days earlier to warn that the Mafia was about to unleash an attack with a car bomb. He said that the target might be Judge Falcone. The police increased the security around Falcone. The Mafia killed Falcone's boss.

It was terrible to live in that city; it was terrible, and tragically normal, to die there. We understood nothing of what was going on. We were swept along by a black inertia, which took us around the city, from one of Death's soundstages to another. In those years, I started to believe that beauty was an antidote to the venom of life: I ingested stronger and stronger doses; I loved beautiful women, and I kept my memories of them, which comfort me in the night when my heart skips a beat. I find, when I think back to all of us back then, that we had a shared sensibility for beauty. There's an injustice in this thought, I'm well aware of it, just as there was that night at the marina, with Sophie, who was the magnetic north of my existential compass. I was attracted to her because I was attracted to life without death. And Palermo was for the most part murderous, a massacre of bodies, ideas, and hopes. I'd like to say that we were taking high doses of love and sex to conquer our fears. It was the first mass anti-Mafia operation in history.

●●●●●

We descended toward the stone wharf, leaving behind us the strains of psychedelic rock. Elena and Paolo were talking about hash, how much better Moroccan hash was than Lebanese hash, finally coming to an agreement on the unequaled black Eden of Afghan and Pakistani hash. Sophie cautiously went down the steps, not because of high heels, which she didn't wear, but because of the darkness into which we were descending. Dim lights illuminated the nets hung out to dry near the bollards.

"*È il mare di notte, senti che odore di calma?*" I asked her in Italian. "It's the sea by night, can you smell the calm?"

She turned around and entrusted me with a sweet glance, and I never knew whether that was out of pure kindness or because she'd inhaled the air and stored up a helping of serenity. The slight sound of the water slapping against the side of the wooden fishing boats added a dose of the surreal to an already surreal setting. It seemed incredible that the little nocturnal paradise that lay before our eyes could be in the same city, the same nation, the same hemisphere where a group of murderers had pressed a button twelve hours ago, unleashing the devastation of people, things, and hopes.

When we reached the far end of the wharf, we looked out at the line of lights ringing the Gulf of Palermo, the reflection of the sliver of moon on the sea, the faint gleam of the lighthouse that marked the entrance to the marina. The spectacle that stretched out before us was reassuring, and inside of me an electric play was being staged. It was the portrayal of a battle: that morning of death versus the evening's emotions; the hard edges of reality against the soft soul of another girl on another night in Palermo. I begged myself for a truce and I got it. I no longer felt my weariness, only the desire to be there, safely offshore, gazing back at that young man in red jeans as he wandered through the rubble and the corpses.

Paolo suggested we lie down and look up at the stars. The stone and cement of the wharf were inexplicably clean, perhaps due to the seawater, which, on the islands, takes the place of absolution and occasionally cleanses things and souls. Elena and Paolo lay down, belly up, making a V with their bodies. Sophie and I imitated them, and we wound up composing an imaginary star; four heads touching: Paolo's dark, bristly head, Elena's neat and glistening black hair, Sophie's blonde locks, and then me, with my tousled dark hair, my tangled beard, my look somewhere between Che Guevara and the Italian actor Massimo Ciavarro.

A starry silence fell over us. I pointed out Ursa Minor to her, sketched it out in the air; she appreciated the gesture even if I didn't know how to say "Ursa Minor" in her language. I tried with various complicated loops of words, which made her laugh. The atmosphere was charged with trust and faith. We were in our twenties and Death, that night, at the exact moment when Sophie turned toward me, had decided to forget about me. She looked straight into my eyes: my memory, my five senses were suddenly recalibrated. It was as if a cat abandoned by the side of a road built only for dogs had suddenly come straight toward me in search of protection.

I once read about Lancelot syndrome, which drives men of all ages to rush to the rescue of any Guinevere who seems to be in danger, whether real or imagined. I didn't know what kind of Guinevere Sophie might be, and I never even had time to ask: we'd been stretched out on that wharf for less than fifteen minutes, and I knew I had to rush to her rescue. Immediately and for the rest of our lives.

Elena and Paolo destroyed our star.

"Let's go smoke a joint on the *Madonna del Lume*."

It was a fifty-foot boat hauled up on the beach, its hull painted by craftsmen who'd cunningly combined the dark-blue enamels with the yellows, the reds, the greens, the whites, and the blacks. The *Madonna del Lume* seemed like a piece of avant-garde art. And it was the highest point around, if you left out the villa of the *tonnara*, where you could smoke a joint.

"Are you coming? *On y va?*" asked Elena, straightening her blouse.

Paolo pulled a pack of blue Rizla rolling papers out of his jeans pockets. My senses were still switched to *off*.

I shook my head imperceptibly; only Sophie noticed that movement, and she, like me, had said nothing. We were staring up at the sky.

"Well?"

"We'll stay here," I said, with that "we" constituting an enormous risk.

"Yes, we'll stay here," said Sophie.

She smiled sweetly at Elena, seeking understanding, and moved her body closer to mine, transforming our star into a pair of chopsticks—she and I, parallel, two pieces of the same wood, bound together on that wharf by a connection that couldn't be broken by the simple force of a pair of hands. We stayed there, watching the other stars. I explained to her that in late July you can see the constellation of Leo, a shape that is impossible to recognize unless you have a book with a star chart within reach, a sort of guidebook to the sky in which, along with the shapes of the stars and planets, you could find the best restaurants on Neptune, the better addresses on Mars, the monuments not to miss on Andromeda—in short, all the best places in the cosmos to spend a romantic weekend.

"Of course, every address is rated, depending on the quality of the service, with a variable number of stars," I added.

Sophie smiled, gave me a light slap on the arm with the back of her hand, and then let it rest there, in a contact that became the light switch governing my senses. They had all just flipped to *on*.

I brushed my fingers, intentionally, shamelessly, against her tapered hand, the hand of a Russian pianist. I felt the elastic consistency of her skin, the long bones, the delicacy of a palm that I could imagine pressed against my chest, in a caress that I was yearning for but that instead was only a dream. Time stopped and took a rest. She shifted her hips to get closer still: the wait was over. I intertwined my fingers with hers, and she turned over on her side to look at me, looking me in the eye with that gaze of hers, a gaze of lake, sea, and ocean. She slowly moved her face closer to mine, I closed my eyes. And she asked me for a cigarette.

I decided to inflict some stupid form of death on myself then and there: like eating twenty pounds of *U pani ca meusa*, or going into an infinite free dive, off Ustica, down down deep, where the brain stops thinking, so that my lungs would pop.

I gave her a Camel and she raised it to her lips without tearing off the filter. I lit it for her; she took two shallow drags and handed it to me: our fingers never separated.

She asked me about my work.

"It's the kind of work you can only do in Sicily," I told her. Then it occurred to me that, actually, I was living in a novel by Dashiell Hammett, and that this city wasn't called Palermo, but Poisonville: a place where everyone died. Always.

She twisted her fingers in mine. She'd heard about the massacre. She couldn't understand it.

"Neither can I."

Then I told her about my friend Fabrizio, my roommate. I told her about how our lives were out of sync: how I woke up at dawn and he got up at ten, how I tried to sleep in the afternoon while he studied, how I stayed out late at night and he went to bed early with his girlfriend, at her place or ours, and in any case in one of two nice middle-class apartments.

My accent was impeccable. I glossed over all the Livias who had passed through our apartment, and through my very comfortable bed, in recent years.

Sophie had never been tense the whole time I'd known her, more than an hour now. She often smiled at my stories, and her laughter was quick and sharp.

She crushed out the Camel on the cement of the wharf. She ran a hand through my hair, and my spine responded. I embraced her, and she crushed her body against mine. She was skinny, and she had small breasts that I could feel pressing naked against my chest. The kiss was long and slow; our tongues met in a single conversation, they shared everything, making delicate gestures of approval, admitting that until that moment they'd never heard anything that made more sense.

We didn't know much about each other. All we knew was that that evening was the start of something.

• • • • •

We left together, Sophie and I. She wasn't used to riding on a Vespa, she didn't know where we were going, but she entrusted herself to my care, and this filled me with joy. The warm night air tousled her short hair; we forgot about Paolo, Elena, and Totino's rock music, we forgot about all the constellations that now seemed to glitter in our eyes, in our hands. She had her arms wrapped around me, clutching me in a way that was at once instinctive and asphyxiating, on the first scooter ride of her life.

"Where I come from we take the metro," she whispered in my ear.

"Luckily we don't have a subway here: you'll have to keep your arms wrapped around me until we get to my house, which is just on the other side of London. It'll take us, oh, two years."

Sophie liked my mix of French and Sicilian, and I was improving in my comprehension of her Norman French. We sailed past Piazza Politeama, which had not yet been defiled by its yellow anti-fog streetlights, designed to fight a fog that Palermo will never see. I slowed down and told her that the perfume she was wearing was a foretaste of paradise. She replied that she never wore perfume.

"Disappointed?"

"I don't know anything about women."

"That's not how it looks to me: you're driving me all over Palermo just two hours after we met."

"Sophie, you're the one who's driving me into the future. We're going to do things together, we're going to talk and talk, we're going to be in love. Do you want a chauffeur?"

"I already have one."

"No, I mean a chauffeur that you can drink. It's a cocktail that's called the *autista*: it's a strange brew, and they make them right around the corner, behind Piazza Politeama."

We wanted to explore each other's bodies on my super-bourgeois bed; it was something we both wanted, and urgently, but it was two in the morning, I'd been on my feet for eighteen hours, and we decided to wait. The bar was called Al Pinguino—the Café Penguin—a name chosen with an unintentional frisson of situationist provocation, considering that it was in a city where the temperature had never dropped below fifty-five degrees Fahrenheit, even during the first Ice Age.

"Two *autisti*, if you please."

The neon lights illuminated the exhausted faces of two men in their forties, unshaven, with sweaty gazes. They were leaning against the counter, drinking beer and soda pop.

The barman squeezed lemon juice into two frosted glasses, added some water and two spoonfuls of bicarbonate, and didn't even need to mix: the foam generated by that mixture overflowed frothily.

"Two *autisti*. I hope you enjoy them."

Sophie shot me a dubious look. I nodded my head yes. We both threw back our drinks, and I understood from the trust she showed as she drank the concoction that this really showed the possibility of becoming a true love affair. Ten minutes later, we were home. Fabrizio was asleep. We made the noises that two people make when they kiss furiously, with the door still open, undressing each other at random, in the front hall, in the living room, and finally in my bedroom, where Maria, the guardian angel who cleaned and tidied the apartment twice a week, had made the bed. The note from Livia was on the nightstand, folded, impossible to read.

Sophie had an elastic body, with a curveless silhouette that was reminiscent of the models in paintings by Schiele. Her natural blonde hair color was highlighted with copper, and she almost had the breasts of an adolescent, with light-colored nipples and areolas. It filled me with tenderness to hold her in my arms, her naked essence.

We made love sweetly, gently, unhurriedly, without any of the urgency we'd displayed as we tore each other's clothes off, victims of that sense of emergency that two human beings experience in the presence of a dangerous fire. Our early adulthood was burning in that embrace, in that demented feverish quest of the other, and then, in contrast, in that slow, rhythmic movement that joined our bodies in the way we whispered, in the way we arched our backs, offering our belly to the world: that is, she offered her belly to me, who, before her, beneath her, and on top of her, became her world, and in that world we recited the eternal prayer of bodies in search of peace.

Sophie's peace came quickly. She cried out something in her language. I right after her, in strangled silence. We lay there motionless, satiated with excitement and deeply moved. I kissed her eyes, I caressed her delicate shoulder blades, her neck—a neck as long as her eyelashes, which only now I was able to see, with our bodies so close to each other, illuminated by the light that filtered through the slats of the shutters. We abandoned ourselves to naked sleep.

The next morning, when we woke up, Sophie asked if she could bring her suitcase, now parked temporarily at Elena's house, to my apartment. I told her yes; I loved that gentle girl. I loved her the way you do when you fall in love with someone instantly, enamored in the most refined form of happiness, direct and without mediation.

I went into the newsroom, and I worked while my mind kept going out to her and wandering back. Her suitcase. What did she have in her suitcase? What does a fashion model take with her when she travels? I didn't have the slightest idea; she seemed like an alien who concentrated in her body all the beauty and all the loveliness of all the universes of Asimov. I supposed that a fashion model must be detached from all earthly concerns, as distant as a strand of silver tinsel carried off by a gust of wind. I hadn't understood a thing.

At work that morning, my boss obliged me to reestablish contact with the control tower on two separate occasions. I was traveling along completely unfamiliar air corridors, I was writing about the Mafia, useless investigations into the car bomb, and the whole time I was thinking about her lips, her taste, the kiss that sex gives and finds, wrapped up in her pelvic thrusts. Sophie controlled her muscles as she pleased; she was an athlete: she danced, she was experienced in runway presentations, and she knew how to master a five-inch stiletto heel. I couldn't wait to get back to her.

At three that afternoon I unlocked the front door to the apartment. The place was dark; no one was home.

I found a note from Fabrizio: "I met Sophie, I made her breakfast. She's very pretty, especially when she's drinking coffee, partially naked. You really are a miserable loser. P.S. She says she's coming back tonight."

I called Elena. She didn't know anything; all she'd heard was that Sophie would swing by sometime that day to pick up her suitcase. Then I tried to get in touch with Paolo. Without luck. I put a record on the turntable: *The Wall*, disc 2, side A, track number 1.

Hey you, would you help me to carry the stone?
Open your heart, I'm coming home.

I was home. Sophie still hadn't opened her heart to me, but I wanted her help.

The afternoon went by quickly, amid a fog of sleepiness with a chemical flavor, heavy as Rohypnol, and a couple of phone interviews that a magazine from up north had asked me to do. I was working from home, in the hope that she'd be there early.

The doorbell rang a little after seven. Palermo was reddened by a summer sunset, with a clear sky, and a thermometer that read ninety degrees. I opened the door for her. She was wearing loose cotton Bermuda shorts and a knit tank top that covered her small breasts. She smiled at me with glowing eyes, dropped her bag, and kissed me on the lips. I hugged her close.

"Come on in, Sophie. You want some juice? A ciggie?"

I helped her stow her suitcase in the bedroom, and she told me that, with Elena's help, she'd gone looking for work, and that she needed a cold shower.

"Room temperature," I corrected her, reminding her that here the temperature was special, feverish.

She smiled, stripped off everything she was wearing, slipped off her panties, strode naked through the living room and the outer bathroom, went into the kitchen, popped open a beer, and told me a little something about the shop where she'd spent her day: in the four minutes that preceded her shower, I learned that the word "modesty" and the word "model" aren't to be found in the same dictionary.

I detected a certain joy in her at being allowed to stay in our apartment, browse through my books and records, with one of Fabrizio's bath towels wrapped around her hips, naked from the waist up, still wet from her shower.

"You have some nice music. Have you ever heard of Francis Cabrel?"

Sure, I'd heard of him. I'd discovered him in Paris four years ago. I had been a student on probation at the Sorbonne Nouvelle, when I was still fantasizing about a future as a linguist. Cabrel is one of those singer-songwriters who in the eighties toyed with women's hearts. He had a gentle, hoarse voice, he belonged to the purest *chansonnier* tradition, and he wrote songs for romantic souls.

Tout ce que j'ai pu écrire
Je l'ai puisé à l'encre de tes yeux.

Everything I've been able to write
Was because I dipped my pen in the ink of your eyes.

I had his first album, purchased in a record shop on the Rive Droite that sold used LPs as well as new ones. I put on track 1, side A. Sophie moved closer to me.

"Not my eyes, the ink of *your* eyes, Sicilian."

She dropped her towel and we made love in the living room. She smelled cool and clean.

We went out to dinner. On Piazza Marina, in the darkness of the quarter known as the Mandamento Tribunali, we found a bistro that a few old comrades from the protest movement had started, people with whom six years earlier I'd founded the first "free radio" in Palermo—and when I say free, I mean free. In just six years, the trajectory from revolutionary to restaurateur had been completed. And to judge from the quality of the eggplant caponata that they were serving, it had ended exceedingly well.

Sophie ate happily, and we both had beers. She told me all about the oily shop owner Elena had introduced her to. The man had suggested she pose for a clothing catalog he was going to distribute to his regional representatives for all of Sicily. She had shown him her portfolio and he had lingered over the photos in which she was closest to nude.

"They don't pay much, but at least…" She never finished her sentence, because I took her hand and kissed it. She repaid the gesture by opening her eyes wide in a look of flattered surprise at finding my lips on her fingers.

"Let's go," she implored.

We paid a reasonable amount for an open-air bistro with paper tablecloths and waiters who asked you: "What'll it be for dessert, comrade?"

It wasn't easy to explain to her, as we left, that for some people it would always be 1968.

• • • • •

The newspaper was buzzing with activity. It was 7:30 in the morning, I had no coffee in my bloodstream, and I'd left Sophie still sleeping in the sheets, damp from the night before. It had finally cooled down just before dawn, when my alarm clock had already begun its countdown. I chose to let her sleep, moving as quietly as a cat that wants something; I threw on any old clothes, that is, the same clothes I usually wore, jeans and a light-colored shirt. I put on my Ray-Bans, grabbed cigarettes, watch, and Vespa keys, and went out the door, leaving the most interesting part of me in that bed next to a girl who, with every square inch of her body, asked me, in her sleep, to stay.

"Sleepy eyes," Saro ribbed me as he usually did when he saw me arrive at the paper. The smile on my face and my wobbly drunkard's gait were both glaring admissions of the facts. I replied: "That's right, my friend, sexy eyes. Worse: the eyes of someone who's in love."

My emotional hangover evaporated on the spot when I stepped into the city newsroom. My boss gave me a scathing glance that lasted three or four thousandths of a second: the longest glance I'd ever received in my life. What had happened? What did he want from me? I could hear three fellow journalists on the phone asking various contacts questions.

"Where? The ring road?"

"When, exactly?"

"Just who found the armory?"

"Have you seen the serial numbers?"

My boss waved me over. I hadn't even reached my desk.

"*Explosives*," he exclaimed, as if he were saying *Buon giorno*.

"Weapons! Get going! As fast as you can! A Mafia arms dump, a veritable armory; there are rifles and submachine guns, half a metric ton of TNT, packets of C4 just like the ones used for the car bomb, semi-automatic pistols. It's the Mafia's entire arsenal. Fuck, get moving!"

He forgot to tell me where; an insignificant detail, an oversight that should never discourage a competent beat reporter. "Where" is something you can always find out; it's the "why" that's harder to track down.

"I'm on my way. When I get there I'll give you a call. I've got plenty of phone tokens; I just hope there's a phone booth."

He shot me one last glance of pity as he tried to calm his nerves by sipping his third triple espresso of the morning, so strong that the sugar wouldn't even sink to the bottom. I galloped down the stairs two steps at a time, and then went back to the doorman's enclosure, where Saro informed me: "Ring road, near the exit for Ciaculli."

I got back on my Vespa. I buzzed out into a Palermo August in the hot year of 1983, already filled to the brim with adrenaline at 7:30 in the morning.

Over the next two hours, Sophie shrank in importance to the level of a character out of a book, a literary figure light-years away from the narrative of things that were happening around me, the creation of another author's pen, in another era, in another novel.

I handled the emotions of policemen with cocaine-crazed eyes, I saw the thirst for vengeance in the eyes of their chiefs and superior officers, I held an Uzi submachine gun in my hands, I learned the difference between a Thompson submachine gun with a standard barrel and a double-barreled over-under sawed-off shotgun. Truth be told, I didn't really understand anything much; I limited myself to drafting a journalistic account of a major find. That's what those years were like: we kept spreadsheets of death, weapons, and none of us were really expected to uncover anything. Investigative journalism was a figure of speech in Sicily in the early eighties. It was a place where Hammett's red harvest really was a bumper crop of blood.

That afternoon I got home, exhausted.

The boiserie was deserted. Sophie had left me a note in French, telling me that she was going back to work for that retailer, at a photo shoot for a catalog.

She showed up at eight o'clock, with a faraway look in her eyes. She gave me a kiss, accompanied by a limp hug, and told me that she was exhausted. All she wanted was a "room temperature" bath. Her skin was luminous, in spite of the fact that Palermo's heat had melted her makeup. She was the most beautiful woman I've ever had eight inches from my heart.

I waited on her hand and foot for fifteen minutes, helping her to put away the clothes and makeup that she'd brought with her for test shots, then I left her alone in the bathtub, immersed in her weariness, in this new, unfamiliar mood.

She emerged half an hour later. She asked me about Fabrizio, did I really want to go out to dinner? I told her no, we could listen to music at home.

"Then help me to relax for real."

She begged me to read her French poetry, saying that she found my Italian accent sexy. She chose the poems of Verlaine, the same poems that her mother used to read to her, in Paris, in their apartment in the nineteenth arrondissement.

She pulled a book out of her bag. I opened it at random. Spleen. I began to read.

Le ciel était trop bleu, trop tendre
La mer trop verte et l'air trop doux.
Je crains toujours,—ce qu'est d'attendre!
Quelque fuite atroce de vous.

The sky was over-sweet and blue
Too melting green the sea did show.
I always fear,—if you but knew!—
From your dear hand some killing blow.

The enchantment of the first day, the first night, the senseless magic of a shared, starry sky: a phantom that materialized then and there, in Verlaine's poetry, sending a shiver down my spine. I, too, feared some killing blow.

Sophie fell asleep a short while later. I listened to her breathing: I could spend the rest of my life inside of her.

The days that followed were a time of nerve-racking routine for me and for her, of *spleen à la façon de Verlaine*. She went out with Elena, who called me afterward to ask me how things were going with Sophie.

"I don't know, we're still making love, but there are moments when she's just not there. That girl..."

"I know; that girl has some black upholstery."

She used a metaphor from the world of car interiors, and I silently shared her point. We said goodbye, promising to get together soon, the four of us, including Paolo, who was fighting day by day his senseless war against adulthood.

We were growing up; we were strong and weak, each to different degrees. Probably Sophie had the highest scores in both rankings.

• • • • •

Handguns and rifles have always played an important role in my life. My grandfather had a gun shop in the historic district of Palermo, just a short walk from the Borsa, or stock exchange, one of the most magnificent and venerable gun shops in the city. When I was a child, every November 2, on the Day of the Dead, he'd give me an air pistol or an air rifle. I've never had a taboo about weapons: I look at them, I caress them, but I don't own them. I grew up with the convictions of a pacifist ready to pull the trigger. I believe that many policemen and carabinieri feel the same way.

In that Mafia armory, where my news editor at the time sent me, I was greeted by the sense of excitement of the officers under the leadership of Commissario Beppe Montana, a young man, intelligent and impassioned. Montana had a feverish gaze, crouching in that culvert that ran under the Palermo-Messina highway, as he was helping his men to pull out the arsenal. We filmed the process with television cameras, and he was happy to let us: in fact, he was a happy man that day. It was a harsh blow to Cosa Nostra; weapons were uncovered that had been used to murder mob bosses and picciotti, but also policemen and judges.

Commissario Montana then went on to lead the Squadra Catturandi, a select team of Mafia-hunters operating inside the mobile squad. He didn't lead it long: on July 28, 1985, on a muggy summer afternoon, he was cut down by two killers sent by the Corleonese outside a shipyard in Porticello, a dozen miles from

Palermo. He'd gone for a drive with his fiancée and a couple of friends. He was thirty-four years old.

• • • • •

"I ran away from Paris. There was a boy who was making my life a living hell…Yes, it's true, I studied under Béjart in Brussels, I paid for the course with a year's worth of savings: I had worked on two major campaigns, for Jean Patou and Kenzo. My mother told me that I just had to watch out for men, they all think that models are human beings in a display case, souls for sale…she hates the people you encounter in my line of work, especially the ones who buzz around the outskirts. There was one I remember, the assistant to a renowned photographer, an incredibly handsome young man from Lyons, who had just moved to Paris. You know the kind of guy I mean, with dark curly hair and a perpetual scowl? I liked him, he courted me the whole time we were shooting for Jean Patou, he asked me out to dinner, I accepted the invitation, and I accepted the consequences."

That night Sophie talked, curled up on the sofa, while the stereo played a Bowie album she liked as much as I did—*Hunky Dory*, one of the Thin White Duke's masterpieces. She was eager to tell me her story, to try to fit together pieces of the puzzle. A fashion model in Palermo: clearly out of place.

"Meeting Elena was fun, and it allowed me to get away from him. I found him relentless, his insecurity, his jealousy, his insistence on being the center of attention every single night. I was just doing my best to work hard, find a little scrap of security. And I was succeeding, but I had to get away from him. An English model I confided in heard that I loved dance, and she mentioned this school of Béjart's. I decided to take a little time off, do a three-month course, and in May I ran away from Paris. That was where I met Elena, and after that it was easy to come down to Sicily. I knew that there was a city here called Cefalù, where they have one of the most fashionable Club Meds on earth, and we French think of Club Med as a little piece of heaven."

I let her talk; I asked no questions. She was different from her usual self. She was loose, she was stroking my hand with the intimacy of a girlfriend, then she lit one of my Camels, and every now and then she'd kiss me, pressing her lips against mine, as if she were getting away with something. Furtive, light. Then she'd laugh.

I'd never seen Sophie that way. I sort of liked it, though in some corner of my mind, something imperceptible, an object out of place in the background, caught my eye. Too many words, certain unfamiliar gestures, her relaxed, jovial tone of voice, nothing in common with the girl steeped in seduction, wrapped in mystery. I imagined French disappointments in a metro station, abandonments, the emptiness of a missing father, and the fullness of a mother absent by necessity. Working in a Paris that to me was legendary but to her was the red zone of suffering. Then her work, the certainty that she was desired, frank and open sex, and finally running headlong to escape from an obsessed man. Coming to Sicily was like catching a ride, out hitchhiking on the highway of life.

I wasn't jealous, I just wanted to understand better. There were vipers in the warm nest of that Sicilian summer and I knew it. In the meantime, I looked at her and desired her. Sophie stripped bare every impulse I had simply by being close to me. I had a constant desire to enter her.

The apartment had become our bed. We made love everywhere, without a second thought, without protection. We took affection for sex, and we took sex for life. That's how it worked, with Sophie and me. We lived. Our life was an attraction out of the animal kingdom, pure subtraction from the intellect. We were different, we were the same. I felt all the tenderness available to me, and in my hands she seemed to be defenseless; I could crush her if I squeezed. Not that night. And I asked myself the question that you should never ask yourself: Why not?

Two days later, Fabrizio found out the reason. We were in the kitchen in the late afternoon. He was in a robe; I was in a T-shirt and jeans. Fabrizio was opening a yogurt.

"Sophie's *shooting up*."

"What are you telling me, Fabri?"

"I found syringes in the trash can in the bathroom."

"What do you think she's shooting?"

"If you ask me, heroin."

"That's not possible, she's not the type."

Two friends of mine had overdosed and died, four years before. I knew a lot about smack: burglaries, thefts, broken windows and stolen car radios, the rapid slide down the ladder of existence, turning tricks for a baggie, lying about everything, with the blank look of idiotic automatons. Sophie was different; two nights ago she'd been so happy, with that urge to talk.

"If she were strung out on heroin, she'd be down, remote, and lackluster. I don't believe you, plus I know her body, I've kissed her arms a thousand times. I'd have seen something. You're talking nonsense."

"In the syringes there was blood mixed with some kind of liquid. She threw them in the trash, relying on our naivete, or perhaps on your being a complete asshole."

Heroin had devastated the sixties protest movement; it had been the far shore for far too many disappointments, the venue in which to elaborate the defeats of life in a self-destructive fashion: we hadn't revolutionized the world, we hadn't changed a thing, but on the other hand, we'd become excellent customers for the Mafia's pushers. A splendid success. But Sophie was a fashion model, she was twenty-one years old, she came from a planet where the word "politics" hadn't been invented yet. What did she have to do with heroin? Fabrizio had found two syringes. He showed them to me: you could see the traces of blood. I said nothing, but I could just hear the dull thump of a fallen body, in free fall for twenty stories, from the top of my soul to the bottom. Sophie falling, crashing to the cement, as beautiful as she was, the central panel in Leonardo da Vinci's codex of proportions, luminous as a fire that burns every word, every conversation; a perfect girl who was becoming a perfect stew of herself. I didn't know how I could go on loving her: I hated heroin, considered it the closest thing there was to a sawed-off shotgun, the sordid weapon that the Mafia used to eliminate its potential enemies. And Sophie was a shotgun shell, cocked and loaded, a pistol aimed straight at me.

I asked myself a number of fairly standard questions: Why hadn't I noticed? Why, if she was strung out, did she still feel like having sex? Who was selling her the smack? How was she paying for it?

I only barely managed to find an answer to the first question: because I'm an asshole. Fabrizio was right: the reason I hadn't noticed was because I was in love. The rest was a mystery that I was determined to solve.

The afternoon that my eyes were opened, that Fabrizio showed me the syringe, Sophie was working: she was shooting the last photographs for the catalog for that fashion boutique on Via Libertà.

The doorbell rang. I went to see who it was.

It was Sophie.

She gave me a kiss on the lips. She smelled faintly of smoke and her mouth was a place where I would gladly have been buried.

"*Ciao*. I'm exhausted."

She had an underlying fair-skinned pallor, heightened by foundation, eye shadow, and mascara, all enhancing her whiteness. They wanted her to look like an extraterrestrial compared with the Sicilian model of beauty in those years, exemplified by a B-cup chest, long raven-black hair, and the kind of pelvis women have in real life but rarely in the world of fashion. The exact opposite of her.

"I had to change fifteen times."

"What's he like?"

"The photographer?"

"Right."

"Okay. Not outstanding. He doesn't know much about lighting."

"What about the client?"

"He's rich. Kind of fat."

"What's his name?"

"Salvatore Cincotta. He has a chain of boutiques called Atelier Donna, with outlets all over Sicily: in Marsala, Trapani, Agrigento..."

I waved my hand, signaling that I wasn't interested in details: I was afraid I might seem to be suddenly worried or, even worse, jealous. Afraid to reveal to her, with a remark or silence, what Fabrizio claimed he had discovered.

Sophie avoided any other questions by starting to get undressed. She embraced me as cautiously as a distant relative, and asked me if I'd run some hot water for a bath. She'd been dreaming of soaking for hours, washing away the makeup, forgetting the day.

I heard the water splashing in the tub, and I knew that she was getting ready to take her bath, that she was naked in my bedroom. I opened a beer. I decided to put off any discussion of heroin till later. I was seized by the terror of ruining everything. That night. In my bed.

Half an hour later, Sophie was stretched out on the sofa, smoking a cigarette, her wet hair pulled back, her breasts barely covered by the bathtowel. Crosby, Stills, Nash & Young was spinning on the turntable.

One morning I woke up and I knew you were really gone.

I could feel clearly that Sophie was going, or perhaps was already gone, and it made me angry to know it could have been Salvatore who had plunged her into the throes of heroin, or perhaps someone else she'd met even before I first met her at Vergine Maria. Palermo was a nest of vipers; Palermo was the world capital of heroin trafficking. I'd seen heroin crystalize into existence in a little villa that broke every building code, located on the waterfront in Acqua dei Corsari, half an hour after the Carabinieri raided the place and uncovered the Mafia's largest operating refinery. I was one of the first people to set foot in the place after the raid; I'd been tipped off by a friend who was a Carabinieri captain. The Cosa Nostra chemists and guards had managed to get away, leaving everything in disarray: the heroin-refining process and their lunch, a fruit salad made of Brazilian oranges, seasoned with oil and vinegar. I noticed a fork stuck into an orange peel in the salad bowl, and I had to think of the misery that man must have felt: after lavishing so much care on preparing this delicacy, he'd had to leave it uneaten, all because of those *cornuti degli sbirri*—those cuckold cops. I sat looking at the beakers and retorts, waiting for the refining process to be finished; I saw crystals form, break, and fall, turning into 100 percent pure heroin: undiluted heroin, capable of killing a junkie with the first push of the plunger into the syringe. As the crystals formed and fell, they made a crackling sound. A sound I'll never forget.

At that exact moment, Sophie, or at least the love I felt for her, started to crack and shatter just like those crystals.

And that's when I started to turn into an executioner.

• • • • •

I hated to think that Fabrizio might be right, that Sophie lived a double life, one in her relations with me and one with the world itself. Was she ashamed of her addiction? Did she not trust me? Or was I her only island of love and purity? Whatever the case, she had refused to tell me the truth, and unless I misremember, truth was the only accepted religion for our generation.

Why wasn't she telling me?

I repeated the forbidden question in my mind: Why not?

I wished everything could go back to the way it was that first night, the enchantment of a boy and a girl bathing their souls in the dark sea of the stars overhead, in the hopes of finding something absolute.

Her.

Me.

Her hand, the hand of a Russian pianist, was pressed against my chest, our tongues were touching, I got an erection at the mere sight of her, the simple contact of her flesh with mine. Her lake-blue eyes—sea-blue, ocean-blue—were leveled at me; around us was the rest of the world: an insignificant landscape.

Now there she was, leafing through magazines on the sofa. Smoking a cigarette, waiting for the city heat to finish drying her off. My trust, however, was gone.

That morning I had read in the newspaper that the main conduit for infection with the new disease known as AIDS was homosexual sex. In second place, heroin addiction. A doctor was explaining that if you were an addict, the only way to reduce the level of risk was to buy and use new syringes every time you shot up, never to lend syringes to anyone else, and never to accept used syringes from anyone. If you were a homosexual, the doctor recommended using prophylactics. A very respectable word, suitable for a mass-audience newspaper. My friends and I had used condoms at the start of our sexual lives, when there weren't many girls choosing to use IUDs or the pill. I used to buy a brand of condoms called Nulla—literally, "nothing." Using them was intolerable, but we had no alternatives: none of us wanted to become fathers or mothers at age eighteen.

I was pretty sure I still had half a box of condoms left over from an affair with a young bookseller that had lasted a couple of weeks. I pulled one out and hid it under my pillow: I had confidently taken a second step down the staircase that leads from worthy to worthless.

I went back to where Sophie was, and she gave me a warm look. She'd recovered. She asked me if I wanted to go out.

"No, I want to stay home, just the two of us," I said, without a smile, without concealing my new state of mind.

I didn't want anything else, just to take her right then and there. I was filled with a dull, aching anger.

She raised no objections, complying placidly. I told her that I'd make her some pasta with botargo— *pasta con la bottarga*; I used parsley, garlic, and fresh red chili peppers. And, of course, the tuna roe that I bought at the Vucciria market from a shady character who claimed he made it with his own hands.

"It's all okay," I added, for no clear reason.

It was a little past eight o'clock on a late-August Wednesday night, and with all the precision of an astronomer, I could pinpoint the beginning of the final clash between two stars on the verge of destroying each other to the moment I said that phrase: "It's all okay." Two stars: Sophie with her heroin, me with my cowardly lies.

"Okay, let's try your *spaghetti avec la botargue*," she smiled, unsuspecting.

She came toward me, wrapped her arms around me with a renewed strength. I grabbed her ass with both hands, possibly a little too vigorously. She didn't care; she gave me a slow, deep kiss.

I urgently desired her blonde pudendum. I felt a yearning to paint over my need for light, to deaden the itch to know more.

I lifted her off the ground, her arms still wrapped around me, half naked. I carried her into my bedroom. She took off my shirt, while I kicked away jeans and underwear in a single motion. She looked at me, restoring in me the desire that she could sense in my unfamiliar new acts of brutality. Her eyes opened wide, softening the features of her face in a smile that was no less erotic. She was intense, warm, and silent. She had opened her pale, elegant legs, the flesh taut over the long muscles, her pubic mound shaved almost smooth, adolescent, a pubic mound that could have persuaded Courbet to give up painting: the origin of the world was blonde, not dark-haired. To understand that, it would have been sufficient to look at Sophie at that moment, the way I did, ecstatic and furious at the same time. The open conflict raging inside me was still there, unresolved. I made myself wait. And I kept myself from penetrating her. I left her standing in a vulgar state of standby, stretched out naked on my bed, me eight inches away from her, our eyes locked.

Sophie must have assumed I was being playful. There was no real foreplay between us: we had the physical urgency of twenty-year-olds; we could make love at the movies, behind a breakwater, in a dressing room at an UPIM department store. Sex on the fly, bound together by reciprocal need.

With my right hand I found the condom underneath the pillow; I slipped it on without ever breaking eye contact. My reaching and stretching hadn't alarmed her, she continued to trust in that young man who hadn't figured anything out, who loved her, period, perhaps the first such encounter in her life where the arithmetic of self-interest hadn't played a role. I slipped on the condom, and I slipped into her. And she screamed.

A powerful scream, something out of Hitchcock, the scream of someone who'd been stabbed. She jerked away from me and I suddenly found myself ejected, with that nothing between my legs dangling in thin air. Then a simple phrase, repeated in a crescendo: *"Je ne suis pas une putain! Je ne suis pas une putain! Pourquoi? Pourquoi?"* Over and over again: "I'm not a whore! Why?"

I mumbled a string of excuses, I talked about the risk of having babies, I begged her to forgive me. She went into the bathroom and locked the door behind her. I leaned against the door and listened to her sobbing softly on the other side.

"Sophie, please, open the door."

The only answer was the splash of the tub filling with water.

Deep within her, a parallel tragedy had just been consummated. Heroin, whore. The two tracks down which her life was running: the demands of drug-dealing pimps the world over, the hungry yearning to seize the opportunity of a beautiful, penniless woman who was also a heroin addict. An ideal victim. With my hypocritical act, the product of male selfishness, I had reminded her just how much of a victim she was. In all her indubitable perfection.

I went back to my bedroom, stretched out, and waited for her to find it within herself to forgive me for my sheer vulgarity. I couldn't think of anything but my own selfishness. A foolish question dictated by the blindness of love made its way into my mind: What if Fabrizio had been wrong?

I pulled her suitcase out from under the bed. I opened it and rummaged through, finding clothing, pairs of panties, a book by Verlaine, various skin creams, a couple of letters from her grandmother postmarked Deauville, three new insulin syringes. I zipped it shut and pushed the bag back under the bedframe. Sophie had locked herself in the bathroom. I waited for her to come out and then, after an hour or so, fell asleep.

In my dreams, I saw her, abandoned, under the Pont Neuf. My arms reached out to her, standing on the deck of a Parisian *bateau mouche*, a tourist glimpsing the life of an enchanting and desperate young woman, in the vain hope of catching her in passing, rescuing her from her fate. In my dream, Sophie's eyes were glazed over, filmy, and she looked at me with the detachment of the terminally ill.

At four in the morning, Fabrizio walked into my room, waking me up.

"Get up and come with me. Sophie. In the bathroom."

"What is it, Fabri?"

"Just come with me."

I imagined the most obvious thing to imagine. I followed him with a piece of tumultuous heart, the only shred left to me: the rest was a dog's breakfast. The bathroom door was ajar, and Sophie was immersed in a tub full of water.

The water was transparent, no streaks of blood, no sign of razor blades. I touched Sophie and woke her up; she was ice cold. She reacted by saying something to me that I couldn't understand. On the floor by the tub was the hypodermic she'd used to shoot up. Luckily, before getting in the water, she'd left the door ajar. Her nudity made her look small, cadaverous, completely defenseless.

I gave her my bathrobe and helped her to my bed.

She fell asleep on her side, her back to me, far away. I decided that I wouldn't go to work the next day. I left a message with the newspaper switchboard in the middle of the night, saying that I had a fever. It was partly true.

When we woke up, any remaining barriers of hypocrisy were gone. I asked the most useless question possible: "Why, Sophie?"

"Just because."

"It'll kill you."

"I don't give a shit. I just want to feel okay right now. Do you have a problem with that?"

I asked a few other questions, of a more technical nature: who, where, when. She decided to tell me what I wanted to know, in a remote tone of voice, as if she were talking about someone else.

"That Salvatore gives it to me, but I also get it from a guy I met the first few days I was in Palermo. He's an aristocrat, and aristocrats always have baggies of smack. I met him through a friend of Elena's. I was already shooting up in Paris, with that photographer I ran away from. He lived to shoot up. I wanted to know if there was another possibility: Brussels, Elena. I was sure I'd be able to do it."

"But then you started it up again. Why, Sophie?" I asked, sticking with the theme of pointlessness.

She shrugged.

"That's just the way I am."

She stopped talking. She prepared her bag for the day's work. I stopped asking questions. She didn't say goodbye, just closed the door behind her. She didn't have a set of house keys; she'd never asked for them, I'd never offered.

That afternoon I had a long talk with Fabrizio. I told him about my conversation with Sophie, her confessions. And that guy, Salvatore, and the nobleman whose identity we were able to guess.

We decided that the summer was over and, whatever else we did, we needed to take a holiday. A long rest from Palermo, a vacation from death and heroin. September was the month for travel, just him and me. We'd taken our first trip together when we were eighteen, after finishing high school. That very afternoon we decided where we'd go: Amsterdam. For a month.

"What about Sophie?"

We agreed that we couldn't leave her alone in the apartment. We knew what drug addicts were like. At that moment, I took a few more steps down the ladder that leads from worthy to worthless. And they were not to be the last.

"I'll make some phone calls. I'll see if there's someone who can take her in."

Fabrizio considered that a wise idea.

That night, Sophie came home. She barely said hello.

She went into the bedroom and lay down.

Almost everything between us was broken. I was afraid of that girl, I wanted to get rid of her, get her far away from me, from my life, her and her syringes, like a handgun aimed at me with the safety off. Then I felt her heart against mine, I'd look at her face, her eyelashes, the lips I would have been glad to dive into and drown. She was still essentially a woman in danger, a Guinevere among Guineveres, and that fact summoned me imperiously back to my duty. I couldn't. I shouldn't.

Lancelot syndrome.

I went into the living room and I called Vittorio. I'd met him at more than one party: he was a skinny, wealthy man, much older than me, born into an excellent family, with plenty of real estate to spare. I told him about Sophie, about the fact that I was leaving, and asked him if he could take her in for a month or so.

"We'll come get her as soon as we get back."

I neglected to tell him about the heroin. Vittorio had seen Sophie at a dinner party with Elena, and during our phone conversation he'd referred more than once to her as that *"bellissima francese."*

He agreed to take her in.

I hung up the phone.

Lancelot had just shot himself in the head.

• • • • •

There was something inexplicable there, just as there is in any self-destructive gesture. In the years that followed, I tried to review the cowardice of that period, the decision to get rid of Sophie as if I were flicking a speck of fluff off a navy-blue blazer. I was a conflicted young man, capable of witnessing an autopsy impassively, or evaluating the effects of a .357 bullet on a human cranium, but incapable of talking to an addict whom I loved, or at least I thought I loved. A drug addict who, at that very moment, was the most defenseless young woman on earth, a tiny creature glimpsed on open terrain by a bird of prey: life. I wasn't indulgent with myself in the months that followed. Then, after a number of years, I grasped what I ought to have understood then and there: I was just a kid immersed in a reality that nowadays would have been a bloodthirsty video game. An avatar moved by the joystick of chance, incapable of decisions and actions guided by a sense of justice.

Sophie continued along her way through the shadows, doing

her best to escape the swooping talons of life for as long as she could. I hurried away from the clearing, in search of a small salvation in the distance that separated me from her. These were natural acts, dictated by the instinct for survival: she had hidden from me the fact that she was a heroin addict, and I had concealed from her the fact that I still wanted the future that was mine by right.

• • • • •

We said our hasty farewells. I borrowed Fabrizio's Renault 4, did my best not to look her in the eye, and put her suitcase in the back. Sophie let herself be transported as if she were a package, putting up no resistance, final recipient unknown; she knew she'd made a mistake, that she surfed through life and had taken another spill. The wave of that Palermo summer had washed over her, knocking her down hard: she didn't expect her weakness to be punished so harshly by the same young man who had described the Baedeker of the stars to her, who kissed her on the eyes and read her Verlaine, the boy in whose arms she had curled up and snuggled. She, the little French girl tossed here and there by the wind.

I delivered her to Vittorio on an afternoon in early September. She was wearing a white tank and linen Bermuda shorts, with a pair of Converse All Stars on her feet. She'd made up her face, red lipstick, mascara to lengthen her eyelashes. She was heartbreakingly beautiful. I was ashamed of myself, of my lack of courage. Sophie entrusted me with one last commiserating glance. I tried to kiss her on the cheek, but she turned her face away. I drove off staring into the rearview mirror: I saw Vittorio picking up her bag as she trailed along after him. Then she turned for a moment to watch my car as it vanished into the distance. The sun picked out the red of her lips.

•••••

Nine years later, in 1992, Giovanni Falcone and Paolo Borsel-lino were killed in Palermo. I worked on both massacres without uncovering anything interesting. Then, over a dinner one night, I discovered another murder; the victim was a fragile and touchingly beautiful young woman killed in Paris by a heart attack: Sophie.

VITO
A Marriage

Blood ties are stronger than a scirocco wind, deeper than the abyss: they are something primordial, something that comes out of nature. A Sicilian knows it from birth, from the first time that, without really understanding it, he experiences the sacred quality of a mother's touch, a father's voice. Of course, everyone else knows it, too, whether born farther north or to the south. But many Sicilians, in all their charming conceitedness, are convinced that the world's most dominant blood type is type S. Not type O, type A, type B, or type AB, but type S: "S" as in Sicily. Their diversity, their imagined supremacy, often makes Sicilians easily recognizable wherever they live. There's an old statistic that said that there were 5.5 million Sicilians living on the island, but there were 15 million more scattered around the world. A great many more than the Irish.

These days, I feel that tie myself, perhaps because I've lived far from Palermo for almost thirty years now. Or else because on certain foggy mornings I feel a yearning for that original light, for wind and the smell of salt water: I have drops of seawater in the double helix of my DNA.

Life takes us elsewhere, we chase after dreams and then, one day, we dream of life. In 1958 Leonardo Sciascia described a Sicilian office worker who was told that he was being transferred: he'd leave his job in a small town and move to a city. But, the official hastened to tell him, he'd make sure the man was transferred to a city nearby. "No," said the office worker, "I'd prefer if it was a city far away: somewhere outside of Sicily, a big city." "Why do you want that?" the official asked in astonishment. "I want to see new things," said the office worker.

Vito's family didn't want to see new things, because it was sealed in an emotional sarcophagus: a grave-like existence made up of rigid borders, dull anger, and misguided loves.

"City newsroom?"

"Yes, go ahead."

"A man named Vito Carriglio *ha fatto scomparsi*—has *disappeared*—his three children."

"Who's speaking?"

"Makes no difference. You write that down?"

My pen was scratching spastically across the notepad. First I wrote *Carriglio*. Then, under that, *Vito*. With my doctor's handwriting, the words looked like a sketch by Jackson Pollock.

"So, you wrote it down?"

"Yes, but…"

Click.

The man had a voice like a dried walnut: hard and wrinkled.

I stood up and went to see my boss.

"An anonymous phone tip, called in in a fine Sicilian accent, reports three children gone missing and accuses the father, a certain Vito Carriglio."

The news editor was stirring his third espresso of the afternoon in a heavy porcelain demitasse: five stirs, six stirs, seven stirs. He was looking at me but said nothing. Eight stirs, nine stirs. I remember reading once that the stirring motion of a cup of espresso can prove hypnotic to some: an

American actor, working at Cinecittà, once stirred his coffee forty-one times, later explaining that the act of stirring had given him a sense of perfection. He drank his espresso cold. The director had been satisfied with the emotional depth of his performance.

But now the news editor stopped stirring.

"So?"

"So what, boss?" I asked, intimidated.

"Have you checked with the archives? Have you talked to the police?"

"No, but—"

"Then why are you standing here busting my balls? Check out the tip and then we'll have something to talk about. There are crazy people everywhere, never forget that."

Good point. Still, that voice like a dried walnut told me that something must have happened.

I phoned down to the archives. Annamaria Florio answered the phone. She was a Marxist-Leninist militant in her forties, and on her days off she stood outside the lobby door of the newspaper, selling copies of *Armare il Popolo,* an insurrectional publication that was usually printed out of register. I'd occasionally buy a copy because she was a friend, but I was pretty sure all the same that the revolution was destined to fail because of defective printing.

"Anna, do you happen to know if we have anything on a certain Vito Carriglio?"

"Hold on. Carriglio, double 'r'..."

I could hear the rustling of the manila folders that contained newspaper clippings and photographs.

"Caronia, Carotenuto, Carraro...ah, here it is: Carriglio. There's nothing here but a photograph. I'll send it up."

Five minutes later a newspaper messenger boy set an envelope down on my desk. I pulled out the photograph. It showed an overweight man, about forty, on his back in a hospital bed, laughing as he held up a bulletproof vest for the photographer to see, as if it were a trophy. His right leg and left arm had been bandaged. There was something buffoonish about his face. He looked as if he was trying to ridicule someone or something.

On the back of the photograph was written: "Vito Carriglio—Ospedale Buccheri la Ferla—October 1982." Underneath that was the stamped name of the photographer, Filippo Lombardo. And the logo of the newspaper.

Up on the fifth floor were the offices our photographers worked out of. Filippo was their chief, a man who roamed the city incessantly, bearing witness to the essence of this slaughterhouse of a city of ours with the direct power of pictures. Murders took place in the street, and then they wound up on one of his negatives. Or else they'd never been committed.

I called his extension.

"Filippo, my lad, do you remember a guy named Carriglio? You took his picture last year."

"Wait, who?"

"It was at the hospital, at the Ospedale Buccheri la Ferla, he'd been shot and he had a bulletproof vest."

"An ugly customer. I remember him."

"Then come on down and tell me all about him."

Filippo picked up the photograph and tapped the nail of his right middle finger on it.

"This one is *tinto*, dark and evil," he said, "the genuine article."

"What did he tell you?"

"Nothing. He didn't want to tell anybody anything, not even the police, but he had no problems with having his picture taken. I asked if he'd show us the bulletproof vest that saved his life. He was laughing and his eyes looked like he was on cocaine: he picked up the vest and I took the picture."

"Did they shoot him in the body?"

"No, they intentionally hit him in the legs and arms. But I did find out one thing: he told a male nurse that for days he'd been wearing that vest around his neighborhood. If I'm not misremembering, he was from Acqua dei Corsari. Can you just see it, someone wandering around on the streets in front of his apartment building, strolling by the seaside, in that getup?"

"You might take him for a nut."

"But then they shoot him, turns out he's not a nut. Anything but, in fact."

"Yeah, but if they'd been out to kill him, they would have shot him in the head."

Filippo gave me a look and started fooling around with the focus ring on his Nikon FM2.

"Legs and arms. That was a warning."

He'd focused clearly.

I went back to my news editor and told him about the shooting and the impressions that Filippo conveyed to me. I repeated his words: "An ugly customer." My boss told me to talk to the police and keep working on it.

The first thing to do was find out whether, by any chance, a missing persons report for three children had been lodged in the past few days. I decided to call the head of the mobile squad, Antonio Gualtieri, a cop from up north, Turin, who'd come down to Palermo two years earlier. We—journalists, investigators, medical examiners, press photographers—had achieved a sort of symbiosis: we'd see one another at crime scenes and exchange rapid greetings and remarks, communications in code, comrades in arms swapping minor confidences. Gualtieri was a short, tough man, disinclined to camaraderie, with the manners of a K9 Corps dog trainer. At first glance, a man to be afraid of, not a man with whom you'd want to establish symbiosis of any kind; but shift the topic to the Juventus soccer team, and Gualtieri would melt like a granita in the summer heat on Lipari. And ever since Unione Sportiva Città di Palermo, the city's soccer team, had sunk out of major league sight and was on the verge of dropping to the depths of Serie C, Palermo had been rooting for the Old Lady, Juventus. As a result, even the grim Gualtieri felt at home. Like a granita on Lipari.

I checked my watch. There would be time to check out those details later. I threw on my fatigue jacket, kick-started my Vespa, and buzzed home to see Cicova, Fabrizio, and his new girlfriend, Serena, who'd just flown down from Milan that afternoon.

• • • • •

I opened the door and the scent of *pasta con i broccoli arriminati*—pasta with cauliflower sauce—washed over me. Fabrizio didn't cook that often, but when he set himself to it he reminded me that divinity could be found hiding in even a simple sauté.

Serena came to greet me, throwing her arms around my neck.

"*Ciao*, journalist."

Her eyes glowed in the dim light of the front hall. They were dark and luminous, a rare case of pure oxymoron, with long lashes. Serena had a physical impact on the world: she touched people, she attracted attention, she looked at people decisively, she didn't mind people brushing against her. Her voice, made up of broad vowel sounds and a Lombard drawl, was softened by her pseudo-French "r." She embodied all the best things about a northern Italy that to us was as distant as Andromeda, far away and mythical. Among its inhabitants, Fabrizio and I were for the most part acquainted with the female offspring, the young women who passed through Palermo on their holidays and often, in those days and in those years, in those half hours, found themselves biting into a cinnamon and Chantilly rice *pezzo duro* Da Ilardo, under the Passeggiata delle Cattive, some of the finest gelato available.

We were living the carefree lives of people in their twenties, immersed in a city that was methodically going about committing suicide.

"*Ciao*, art historian," I replied.

Our embrace dissolved slowly, giving us both all the time we needed to explore each other's backs and shoulders, inch by inch. I hadn't seen her for a month. I loved her dearly: she was my best friend's new girlfriend.

We had met that summer on Vulcano, on the Sables Noirs, the obsidian beach on the west side of the island. Serena was on holiday with her two girlfriends, while Fabrizio and I were taking a short break during a working August: I was busy describing corpses; Fabrizio was reviewing various subjects in preparation for overview exams.

The only brunette of the three women was Serena, and she was also the prettiest. With the nicest smile, and the most attractive tan. The finest topless. Valentina and Alba, her two blonde, blue-eyed friends, vied to make friends with me: neither of them was forced to concede defeat. Serena aimed straight at Fabrizio's heart. She, too, emerged victorious. Those ten days on Vulcano left a decisive mark in the emotional pavement of our lives.

"Where have you been, girl of the north?"

"Home. With my folks. But now I'm going to stay with you guys until Christmas."

"And your exams?"

"They're in February. Seventeenth-century art. Applied arts. Studying down here is like getting extra summer: Fabrizio, you, the warmth in the air…"

Cicova had come over and was rubbing against my legs. Demanding attention. Serena leaned down to stroke him. He started stretching, his whole body purring.

"Let's go see the cook," she said.

I tossed my fatigue jacket on one of the sandalwood chairs that adorned the front hall and followed her into the kitchen.

● ● ● ● ●

"I want to file a criminal complaint."

"Theft?"

"Theft of children."

The patrolman standing guard at police headquarters sized up the petite woman looking up at him. He noticed her decidedly unfriendly eyes.

"Third floor. Complaints office. You'll find one of my colleagues; tell him that this isn't about cars or jewelry."

He adjusted his regulation cap and the knot of his tie. He wasn't sure what kind of reaction to expect. The woman went on looking at him, expressionless. She was dressed in a nondescript manner: a light cotton jacket, dark brown, over a beige skirt, low-heeled shoes, taupe-gray stockings. Her face looked as if it had been sketched by a Cubist painter: all angles, with thin lips, ash-gray eyes, and an aquiline nose.

"All right," she said. "Third floor."

A young policeman with a Roman accent greeted the woman with a distracted "How can I help you?" uttered in a vaguely questioning tone.

"I'm here to report that my ex-husband has taken my three children and I haven't seen him since."

"Go see Inspector Zoller: down that hall, first office on your right."

The woman knocked on the door.

A weary "Come in" authorized the woman to open the door.

Inside was a man in civilian clothing, about 225 pounds, with an enormous salt-and-pepper mustache. "What's this about?"

"I'm here to report the disappearance of my children. I think that my husband has taken them."

Inspector Zoller pulled a handkerchief out of his trouser pocket and mopped his forehead. October at the thirty-eighth parallel of latitude was like August at the forty-seventh parallel: he knew it, he'd always known it, they'd explained it to him in his geography classes, but rediscovering it every year, after twenty years of duty in Palermo, always caused a certain annoyance.

"Sit down and give me some ID."

The woman opened a patent-leather handbag with a fake gold clasp. She pulled out her identity card. The inspector read aloud: "Savasta, Rosaria, born in Palermo on June 27, 1953, residing, also in Palermo, at Via Ettore li Gotti, 11. Do you confirm?"

"That's me."

"Let's continue: tell me briefly the content of your complaint."

"My husband and I, my ex-husband even if we aren't yet legally divorced, his name is Vito Carriglio; well, my husband and I had agreed that he could see them twice a month, Saturday and Sunday. He picked them up last Saturday, at ten in the morning, and today is Wednesday, and I still don't know anything about him or about my children."

"What are the children's names?"

"Giuseppe Carriglio, Salvatore Carriglio, and Costanza Carriglio: twelve, ten, and six years old."

"Have you gone to look at your husband's place of residence?"

"Of course."

Rosaria Savasta shot the human mountain that sat before her an angry glare: you should never question the intelligence of a Sicilian woman. Especially if the woman in question is the daughter of the mob boss Giuseppe Savasta, aka "Tempesta," and she's turning to the police, thus breaking one of the most inviolable taboos of Cosa Nostra.

The inspector limited himself to taking notes and translating into bureaucratic jargon the fury that the woman was emitting from her ash-gray eyes. A quarter of an hour later, as the bells of the Arab-Norman cathedral rang out the noon hour, Rosaria Savasta was signing the criminal complaint denouncing the disappearance of her three children. She attached the three photographs she had brought with her, anticipating the request that the police were about to make: the daughter of a mob boss always knows what the police are thinking.

At six that evening the head of the mobile squad, Antonio Gualtieri, confirmed that earlier that day a woman had filed a criminal complaint concerning the disappearance of three minors.

"Are they named Carriglio?" I asked immediately.

Gualtieri said nothing at first.

"How do you know that? Did one of my men tell you about it?"

"It's an odd story. I received an anonymous phone call."

"When?"

"Yesterday."

"Come straight over and let's talk about it."

The chief of the mobile squad wasn't interested in commenting on the return to play of the world soccer champions Dino Zoff, Antonio Cabrini, and Paolo "Pablito" Rossi. The game in question was a tougher one.

At 8:30 that evening, after an unspecified number of espressos that would keep me awake until much later that night, we came to the following agreement: I'd tell Gualtieri everything I found out about the case, and he would give me an exclusive account of the actual developments of the investigation. I had a direct line to the anonymous tipster, and my reward for that would be learning everything before the other journalists. I went home feeling satisfied.

• • • • •

Fabrizio was playing his guitar, practicing a piece by Villa-Lobos—a piece that involved an arpeggio that would have sorely tested Houdini. Serena was curled up on the sofa, next to a designer lamp that illuminated her corner of the room: she was reading *The Red and the Black*. Cicova was roaming around the living room in search of any olfactory trail that might lead to food.

All in all, a quiet, bourgeois setting.

"Where have you been?" Fabrizio asked, halting the motion of his fingers on the strings.

"Police headquarters, something boring."

Serena lifted her eyes and looked at me.

"That's good. If it had been something melancholy, you'd be in big trouble," she said.

"What do you mean by that?"

"Listen to what Stendhal has to say." She sat up straight, with the posture of a radio announcer, and started reading with her soft "r": "If you are melancholy, it is because you lack something, because you have failed in something. *That means showing one's inferiority;* if, on the other hand, you are bored, it is only what has made an unsuccessful attempt to please you, which is inferior." Then she laughed. "All right, Sicilians, what's for dinner?"

Villa-Lobos was put away in the guitar case, and I went into the kitchen to open a can of Petreet for Cicova. Then I put a pot of pasta water on to boil.

"*Aglio, olio e muddica atturrata*," I shouted, so they could hear me in the living room. Pasta with garlic, olive oil, and toasted breadcrumbs.

"*Grazie*, journalist," Serena cried in a loud, clear voice.

"If you want, I'm glad to *atturrari la muddica*," said Fabrizio, strolling into the kitchen. It was a matter of slowly toasting some breadcrumbs in a skillet, with a little salt, some olive oil, and, in accordance with a modification I'd made to the recipe two years earlier, a light grating of nutmeg. The breadcrumbs were toasted till they were a dark brown. Then you sprinkled them instead of Parmesan cheese over Tomasello pasta cooked al dente, pasta already flavored with the oil used to sauté, long and low, the garlic and the chopped parsley. I accepted his offer to help. We opened a bottle of Corvo white wine.

After dinner, Simona called. She was a friend of my sister's, and she wanted me to read the beginning of a novel she'd written. I told her to swing by right away, if she wanted. The first few pages were a little boring, but—luckily—not melancholy. I told her it was really great, and her face lit up. After that we made love, and it was sort of sweet.

The next morning, at a quarter to seven, I made breakfast for everyone: coffee, tea, Stella long-life milk, Oro Saiwa cookies, and an open box of Pavesini cookies. I left three mugs on the kitchen table.

While they were still sleeping, I was back on the hunt for Vito Carriglio. Or at least for his wife.

• • • • •

"What did the head of the mobile squad tell you?"

"We can work together. We have an understanding. They'll tell us everything they have, and we'll tell them everything we have."

"What do you know about these people?"

"She's the daughter of a guy who's supposed to be a mob boss. He, the husband, is half a *malacarne*. A Mafia underling, at the very most."

"And just how can it be that the daughter of a mob boss is talking to the police?"

"An act of contempt toward her husband. If she'd just turned to her family it would have been normal; setting the police after him, after this half a *malacarne*, is a terrible punishment."

"Then get busy. I'd like to publish the first article today."

The news editor was leafing through the pages of our main rival, a morning paper. An old-fashioned, conventional broadsheet, which everyone in Palermo looked at for obituaries and wedding announcements: the only two objective parameters to measure the success of a media outlet. We were an afternoon paper, smaller in format, more socially engaged, more combative, smarter, and therefore poorer. A Dickensian poverty: proud and honest.

I set out in search of Rosaria Savasta. The chief of the mobile squad had given me a Xerox of the complaint, with all her information. I found Via Ettore li Gotti on the city map.

Acqua dei Corsari. Just a short distance from the seafront along which Via Messina Marine ran, the coast road that every Saturday of my childhood I drove down with my family in our car, my father, my mother, and my sister, to go to our tiny weekend house in Porticello. I remember the rocky beaches and then the garbage along the Statale, the highway, just outside of Palermo. But at the end of that drive, surrounded by orchards of lemon and orange trees, after we'd passed through villages with names that meant nothing to me—Ficarazzi, Ficarazzelli—we'd come to my own private paradise. The tiny house on the water, with the waves crashing beneath the window of the bedroom where my sister and I slept. That was where I learned everything I know about life: how to swim, how to sail a boat, how to fish, how to protect myself from jellyfish, how to spearfish, how to gut a fish, how to kiss a girl on the wave-swept rocks, how to build a *strummula*—a handmade top that you spin with a length of twine—how to look up at the stars over the water by night, when the lights of the world we lived in, back in the mid-sixties, were so inadequate and faint that they didn't interfere with the daydreams—or nightdreams—of someone trying to find the constellations.

I climbed aboard my Vespa and headed back down that road.

Via Ettore li Gotti was a U-shaped street that ran from Via Messina Marine back to Via Messina Marine. An elbow lined with unsightly buildings from the fifties. Number 11 was a two-story apartment building with crumbling balconies. There was just one buzzer on the main door, with no name by it. I rang the bell. A woman's voice asked who I was. I told her my name: I wanted to talk about the three children.

The only answer was silence.

"Signora Savasta, I really do think I could help you."

The click of the door buzzing open was the final answer.

The whole building belonged to the Savasta-Carriglio family, probably more to the Savasta side than to the Carriglio side.

•••••

The staircase smelled of formaldehyde cleaner. The handrail was made of anodized metal. A petite woman with a sharp-edged, angular face was waiting on the upstairs landing. She studied me as I climbed the last steps leading up to the second floor.

"Signora Savasta?"

"Who are you?"

I told her my name a second time, followed by: "I'm a journalist; I know something about the disappearance of your children."

"Ah": a sound that might mean *Please come in.*

The front hall was dark. I walked in and she closed the door.

"Nothing, it's just a journalist," she said with a glance toward an adjoining room.

"Ah," replied the voice of an older woman.

Then Signora Savasta took another look at me, a less suspicious one this time; this look was nothing more than an invitation to join her in the living room.

From the windows you could see the building across the way: taller, uglier. An oil painting of a clown adorned the wall behind an enormous sofa in the Louis Philippe style. The coffee table in front of the sofa was covered with crayon drawings on construction paper. A pencil case lay beside the drawings. A large television set, in the corner, seemed to evoke the evenings that the kids spent watching it.

The woman, with a slight jut and lift of her chin, directed me to have a seat on the fake Louis Philippe sofa.

"*Grazie.*"

"Now tell me what you know and what you want to find out."

If she was angular before, she was razor-sharp now.

"Signora Savasta, I've received an anonymous phone call about your children."

"And what did the person say?" she asked without revealing a thing.

"That Vito Carriglio has arranged for his three children to disappear."

"That's something I already know."

"Yes, but the person called before you went to police headquarters."

"That damned bastard of a husband of mine," she murmured.

It was starting to dawn on the woman: someone else was in the know.

"Exactly what words did they use?" she asked.

"They said that Vito Carriglio *'ha fatto scomparsi'* his three children. *Disappeared* them."

"Three days ago…*Disappeared* them…"

The sharp angles of her face had hardened into marble. That expression was a bad sign—*disappearing* someone is a phrase they use in the "family" to mean…

"*Signora*, can you tell me what kind of person your husband is?"

"I already told that police inspector from up north. They already knew about him: he's a *fissa*. A guy that in my family is considered a *mafallannu*, someone who doesn't know how to do anything."

"And what do you think of him?"

"I belong to my family."

"But you had three children with somebody like that."

"These things happen," she replied, adjusting her taupe skirt.

I didn't know how to talk her into telling me her story. I understood that she was accustomed to the dominion and silence of power. The daughter of a boss, but married to a *fissa*: I couldn't see why she'd chosen to spend her life with a mediocre loser and a coke hound who walked around town in a bulletproof vest.

"And a year ago they shot him. Shot your husband, I mean."

"Family matters," she replied.

The voice of the older woman, from the next room, asked: "Did you offer him '*u cafè*?"

"No, Assunta." Rosaria Savasta asked me, "Would you like some?" Adding, after a brief pause: "That's my elder sister, who is a *signorina*: she's come to stay with me since Vito took the children away."

"No, *grazie*. Just a little bit of Idrolitina, if you don't mind."

"Assunta, the journalist wants bubbly water. My children like it, too."

Maybe I'd found the first crack in the wall.

"Could you explain to me just what your family is planning to do with Vito?"

"Why should I? Why should I care about you, no offense meant?"

"I might be able to help you: you want to get your children back, and I want to give you a hand. If I find something out, I'll tell you immediately. And I'd expect the same thing from you. That way, I can print the truth in the newspaper I work for."

"My husband doesn't deserve the truth. The truth is for honest people. Someone who steals his children from behind your back is a dishonest coward."

"While the rest of you, your family, prefer honest people."

"My father likes real men, not half-men who pull armed robberies in tobacco shops, get drunk, take drugs until they don't know what they're doing, half-men who raise their hands to their wives…"

Half-men who raise their hands to their wives, a private and concrete action. Like all the actions that marked the code of behavior in the old Cosa Nostra at the end of the seventies: you don't behave like buffoons, you don't take drugs, and you don't beat women. Ever.

She watched me drink the Idrolitina that her sister Assunta had brought me. Assunta was a dried-out old crow with sunken eyes. Rosaria's expression was neutral. The list that she'd made sounded like a succession of offenses from the criminal code, uttered by a bailiff: a distant tone of resentment, the colorless voice of the law.

"And one day my father just got *siddiatu*. Fed up, if you follow me."

"And he had him shot."

"I never said that."

"Fine. Someone shot Vito, and after that he went off to live somewhere else."

"I threw him out of the house myself."

"But you came to an arrangement for him to see the children."

"What could I do: he's still their father, after all."

"Twice a month."

"That's right. He'd come on Saturday morning, they'd go downstairs. And then on Sunday evening they'd come back. I'd ask and they'd say: Papà took us to eat sea urchins, Papà took us to shoot at targets at the fair, Papà bought us cotton candy...I'd ask if he'd done anything odd and they'd tell me that he was always on edge, sweaty, that he wouldn't tell them anything, but he'd always buy them something."

"Had you had any fights recently?"

"Yes, one night. In front of the children. I told him that he couldn't bring them back home to me in that condition: filthy, their clothes a mess, dropping with exhaustion. He told me to keep my mouth shut or he'd kill me. He even slapped me twice in the face, with the children staring at us. Then he left."

"Did you tell your father?"

"What else could I do? Two weeks later, when he came home with the children, my father was here waiting for him. And he said terrible things to Vito, in a calm voice: that Vito wasn't a man, that no one should behave like that, that if he kept behaving that way, then..."

"Then what?"

"Nothing. But Vito's always been afraid of my father. He left then and there, without a word of farewell; let's just say that he took off running."

"Do you know where the children go to sleep on Saturday nights?"

"At my sister-in-law's place. In Passo di Rigano."

"Did you ask her?"

"Certainly."

She looked daggers at me: stupid question, icy answer.

That adverb rang out like a gong. Round over. I thanked her for the Idrolitina and said goodbye, knowing full well that I'd never write a line. That conversation, she'd told me with a glance, as she saw me out, had never taken place.

• • • • •

Judging by appearances, Cosa Nostra has never offered women a particularly important role. It entrusted women to their men, and those men, in turn, entrusted their wives with their own off-spring. A silent matriarchy, which inspired even Giuseppe Tomasi di Lampedusa: the role of Fabrizio Corbera, Prince of Salina, so central to the plot and to historical analysis, is strictly second-ary once the front door of Casa Salina swings shut. And his wife, Maria Stella, is the real head of the family. She knows everything about her husband, all about his weaknesses, and she lets him play, the way you do with a pet cat. Meanwhile, it is she who runs everyone's lives.

Ninetta Bagarella, the younger sister of a bloodthirsty mob boss, Leoluca, was engaged in 1974 to Totò Riina, the best friend of another of her brothers, Calogero. It was a way of strength-ening relations, sealing a bond between families, as well as cre-ating a more powerful military force. Signora Bagarella Riina, described in online encyclopedias as "an Italian schoolteacher and criminal," is a perfect reflection of Sicilian matriarchal pragma-tism. She was well aware of her own role, she married the capo di tutti capi while he was on the run from the law, she gave birth to four children, some of whom are currently guests of the Italian prison system, she was ordered to pay restitution to Judge Borsel-lino's family of 3,365,000 euros, and before every judge she spoke to she always described herself as a woman in love.

Cosa Nostra never applied hiring quotas when it came to women. Cosa Nostra never had to.

• • • • •

"*Ciao*, journalist. Tonight the apartment is a no-man's-land."

"Where's Fabri?"

"Playing soccer. Don't you remember that your friend is an athlete first and a man second?"

Serena was barefoot, wearing a blue-and-white striped man's shirt and white shorts, and her forefinger was marking a page roughly two-thirds of the way through *The Red and the Black*.

"Busy day?"

"We went to Mondello: bread and *panelle* and a stroll on the beach. A seagull followed us, scavenging the crumbs we dropped on the sand. Fabrizio talked to me about next summer. Do you really want to spend a month in France?"

"Paris, more than France. There's a girl…"

"And I'll come with you."

"Is Fabri okay with that?"

"He wants me."

"So do I." I corrected my phrasing: "So do I, want you to come with us to France."

She smiled and set down the book, dog-earing the top right corner of the page.

"Do you know what time he's coming home after soccer?"

"Late: a match and then a pizza with the team. Are you going out?"

"No. I wanted to read, watch TV. Listen to music. I don't know."

"Shall we eat?"

"I can make spaghetti with tuna roe. I bought some just the other day at the Vucciria market."

Serena grabbed me by the hand and dragged me into the kitchen, as if it was an emergency.

"All right then, get to work, journalist. And work quickly, I'm hungry. I want roe, tuna spaghetti, whatever you've got."

I managed to toss my fatigue jacket on the sofa. I washed my hands in the kitchen sink.

"You work, I'll be the DJ."

I recognized the first few notes of Coltrane's "My Favorite Things": piano, string bass, drums. And then the hypnotic sax came in. I loved evenings that emerged out of pure chance and pure jazz.

In fifteen minutes the water was on the boil. Just enough time to grate some tuna roe, heat up some oil in a small pan with red pepper, mince the parsley, choose the spaghetti, set the table, open a can of cat food for Cicova, and find a bottle of white wine in the fridge to polish off.

Serena played at being the guest. I found her sitting at the table, her hair tied back in a ponytail. I knew the weight and texture of her hair, and I liked it. I served her deferentially.

"What did you do today? How many people did you kill?" she asked.

"I just count the dead bodies. There are other people who do the actual work."

"How many?"

"None. But I talked to a woman who's trying to find her children."

"Where did she lose them?"

"Her husband took them, a violent man, half a Mafioso. A troubled family history."

Serena stopped asking. After the spaghetti, she made me look around the house for some rum: "I want to see what it's like."

"Sweetish," I told her, "it's made out of sugar cane. You ought to try some whiskey."

"I don't even like the word. I want something sweet."

I found the rum, tucked away behind a bottle of Yoga peach nectar, in the pantry. A friend of my sister's had brought it one night so he could make us a cocktail that he claimed was described in a book by Hemingway.

Serena took a sip of rum. She made a face like an orchid and looked at me.

"What about you, journalist?"

"The word I like is 'whiskey.' "

I poured myself two fingers of scotch. I sat down on the sofa; Serena took off Coltrane and put on *Kind of Blue*, by Miles Davis. The first piece was like an endless question: "So What." Serena gave me a *so what* look. Well?

She sat down next to me. It was nine o'clock on a warm autumn night. She was wearing a shirt of Fabrizio's and it did little to conceal her naked body underneath. Her breasts weren't big but they had balance and perfection, qualities that right then were picturesque more than erotic. But still.

But still, she was curled up next to me, a little too close to me, and we had two, maybe three hours to endanger our senses. I asked her about Stendhal.

"He teaches you to value love."

She admitted that she'd fallen in love with the character of Julien Sorel. I told her that stories made out of paper and words usually end badly. I quoted from memory, and therefore incorrectly, a phrase of Henry Miller's that I took as a guide in those years: "What doesn't happen in the open street is false: literature."

She smiled, picking up on the sense of reality that I was trying to impart. Then I asked her about seventeenth-century art.

She grimaced. Miles Davis didn't go with Annibale Carracci. And just then, she'd chosen "So What."

"Well, so?"

She looked inside me. The place was a mess.

"So what?" I gulped.

"I'm talking about you. You and other women. That Simona the other night. What are you doing to yourself? Why are you scattering yourself in all directions?"

"I didn't choose. That's the way I like it, that's all; all I want is a night's pleasure, two nights if it's something that seems to be working."

I threw back a swallow of scotch, saying a mental prayer to Humphrey Bogart in *To Have and Have Not*. Serena took my hand: her skin was dry. My heartbeat went all syncopated; Bill Evans was setting the beat on the piano.

"But if I were a girl who'd just come to Palermo on vacation, and if you met me at a party, and if I made you laugh and you made me laugh, and then we came home, here, to this apartment…would you or wouldn't you go to bed with me?"

"But you're Fabrizio's girlfriend."

"Stupid, my question is abstract. Would you or wouldn't you?"

"Is my answer supposed to be abstract?"

"Yes or no?"

"No."

She shot me a challenging look.

"Why not?"

"Because you're Fabrizio's girlfriend. There's nothing abstract about that."

"You really are holding on to reality too hard: a journalist. But you're sweet."

Her breast, poorly concealed by the shirt, seemed to nod in agreement. That breast had to agree. I felt like a fool, but a heroic one. This time, the code of friendship had been honored, which had not always been the case.

Serena let go of my hand, which was damp from my racing heartbeat, while hers remained perfectly dry. She went back to the record player, took off "Blue in Green," and put on a singer who'd performed at the Sanremo Music Festival and who wasn't bad. She chose a track called *"Vita spericolata."* She made me get up from the couch.

"All right, journalist. But at least let's dance."

I tried out a few awkward steps, at a distance from her. I watched the way she moved perfectly, the curve of her hips appearing now and again in the way that her shirt clung to her body, the high, rounded shape of her bottom, framed by her white shorts. She was beautiful, self-confident, dangerous.

Yes, I'd go to bed with you, I thought. And I ran away, with some stupid excuse, and hid in my bedroom.

At eleven o'clock, Fabrizio came home. And our friendship was safe.

• • • • •

I tried to get to sleep, but in vain. I spent a couple of hours tossing and turning, sitting up in bed and reading a book, failing to register a word, tossing the book on the floor. Lights off. Lights on again. One hundred twenty minutes of listening to my own voice, inside my head, telling Serena no. "No. Because you're Fabrizio's girlfriend." A real idiot, and at the same time forthright, heroic. I found Serena far more attractive than Simona or any of the other young women who passed through our apartment during that period. What held me back where she was concerned was a single adversative conjunctive adverb that appeared before my eyes as a gigantic, blinking neon sign, filling my head with its glaring light. A single word, common and everyday: HOWEVER. "I really like Serena a lot, HOWEVER, she's my best friend's girlfriend." I thought about the attraction that could pull a man and a woman together, solid as a porphyry cube, firm to the touch, something you couldn't live without at any moment of your day, a sentimental amulet you carried with you wherever you went, a physical sensation that ran through your muscles, a thought against which you measured all your other thoughts. I felt an attraction as dense as marble for Serena, the concrete substance of my desire. HOWEVER. However, nothing was going to come of it.

In that dream state, half asleep, half awake, filled with overlapping memories, mirrors, and reflected images, I saw myself again that afternoon, at the home of that diminutive, sharp-edged woman. I heard her voice as she told me about the "hands raised" against her. A man feverish with cocaine and madness, beating his own wife, the mother of his children. A violent fool, I thought, but still, half of a married couple. Vito and Rosaria. Just like Fabrizio and Serena. Or me and Serena. Like Simona and me. Different types of attraction, variant forms of love. Some of them unhealthy, others literary or obsessive. I suddenly regained a sense of clarity and I switched on the light. I wasn't sleepy; I was never sleepy in those years in Palermo. A friend of my father's who was a neurologist, whom I'd gone to see the previous summer after nearly fifteen days without sleep, explained to me—making use of a metaphor—that my sleep problems were caused by "a wrinkling of the cerebral cortex." A defensive shrinking, I decided; more or less like what an octopus does when it sees an enemy approaching. It contracts its muscles and the surface of its head becomes rough and compact. I was doing it to defend myself from my own life: the life of a young man, age twenty-four, who came home at night and had to scrape human blood off the soles of his shoes at the front door. An uncommon way of life: varied and profoundly sick.

I turned off the light when I woke up again, at a little after six. I had collapsed under the weight of my own self-pity. In an hour or so I was expected for work at the newspaper. Report everything I'd learned. Make sure that the soles of my shoes left no stains on the linoleum.

• • • • •

The estimate that the writer Enrico Deaglio makes is ten thousand dead in southern Italy, over the course of a decade or so. A little smaller than the number of dead in Kosovo. But NATO intervened in Kosovo. The forces they sent to Palermo, in contrast, were a few cops and some carabinieri. Thousands of people were shot down in cold blood or "disappeared," which means kidnapped and killed, during the second great Mafia war, which broke out in the late 1970s and came to an end in 1993. Bodies that have never been found again, a generation of Mafiosi exterminated, the Italian state left in tatters, an endless list of names before which we can only bow our heads: Boris Giuliano, Gaetano Costa, Piersanti Mattarella, Michele Reina, Pio La Torre, Carlo Alberto Dalla Chiesa, Rocco Chinnici, Emanuele Basile, Mario D'Aleo, Ninni Cassarà, Giovanni Falcone, Paolo Borsellino…judges, honest politicians, policemen, carabinieri. Some of them are well-known throughout Italy, others less so.

Those were years of an undeclared war. Correspondents for the major newspapers were sent to Palermo every once in a while on the kind of random basis that guides the lives of war correspondents on the front line: today Beirut, tomorrow Belfast, the day after tomorrow Palermo, trying to figure out in the few hours available why the Corleonese were no longer allies with the clan of Passo di Rigano. We young journalists watched as the big names came raining down from above on our daily routines, and we thought they were heaven-sent gifts: someone else cares about Palermo, about the world inside this blood-filled aquarium. They flew in, they tried to understand, they filed their articles, they flew away. Then, for those of us left behind, the daily grind of death started up again. One morning, a little before eight, I was sent out to Via Messina Marine to cover a murder: someone had shot a traveling seafood vendor. His stall was little more than a cart with two wheels and a pair of handles, filled that morning with nothing but jumbo shrimp. The fishmonger's dead body lay on the sidewalk, surrounded by shrimp and a large puddle of blood. That image of shrimp bobbing in the blood of the man who sold them was emblazoned in my memory. It seemed to me that the complementary nature of the two shades of red were the epitome of some form of refinement. That was just one more morning when the soles of my shoes were smeared with blood.

• • • • •

The next morning, in the newsroom, I had my first espresso of the day with Matilde, an editor in the entertainment section with whom I'd had a fleeting affair two years earlier. She lived in a two-room apartment on the third floor of a nineteenth-century apartment building overlooking the harbor. The yellow light from the street lamps that lined the waterfront leaked into our nights through the slats of the shutters, casting an egg yolk—hued ladder on the dark wall to the left of her bed. We made love illuminated only by that saffron glow. Then, in the morning, well before seven, we'd leave for the newspaper: she took one route, I took another. We never came in together. At work, we ignored each other. Even at that age we lived undercover, unnecessarily, but driven to it by what the city was teaching us.

That day, as we sipped our coffee together, we chatted idly about the city's political situation. Then she told me about a new play that the theatrical director Michele Corrieri was developing with the young actors of Scenikos: it was going to be based on the Mafia war, but transfigured into a Greek drama. I told her briefly about the investigation I was working on. She caressed my face: the stubble on my cheeks made the gesture somehow less intimate.

I went back to the city newsroom and went into my boss's office. It was 7:10 in the morning and his adrenaline was already up to afternoon levels. He slammed down the receiver and glared at me as if I was parked illegally.

"I talked to Carriglio's wife," I began.

"What did she tell you?"

"That he's a bastard, that he used to beat her, even in front of the kids, and that a year ago her father, Tempesta, had the man shot."

"Did she say it in those exact words?"

"As good as."

"As good as, my ass."

"It doesn't matter, I can't write a word: the conversation with Rosaria Savasta was off the record. It officially never happened."

At that point, my boss was angry enough to write me a parking ticket. He might even have called a tow truck and had me towed.

"So now what?"

"So now I'm going to call the chief of the mobile squad, Gualtieri."

I wouldn't have to. Just then, the guy at the desk next to mine, Roberto Pozzallo, a courts reporter, short, greasy-haired, the son of wealthy farmers, shouted my name, followed by the words: "Hurry! It's Gualtieri on the phone for you!"

The chief of the mobile squad said only a few words: "We've arrested Vito Carriglio." Then he added "*Ciao*," and hung up.

Ten minutes later, I was outside his office door.

"Come right in, the chief is expecting you," said a patrolman sitting at what looked like an elementary shool desk: the top was slightly inclined, in dark wood, with a groove for pencils.

Gualtieri was at his desk and he was toying with the Juventus pennant that he used as a paperweight, set on a small flagstaff planted in a small wooden base.

"We picked up your 'ugly customer' at Santa Flavia. He was in a trattoria; we got a tip from an informant who works in the fishing marina. We took him in for kidnapping a minor."

"What about the children?"

"They weren't there. He wouldn't say a word."

"Have you talked to the wife?"

"Not yet. First I wanted to hear what she had to say to you. I know you went to see her," he said, putting down the pennant.

I'd already guessed that he'd had me followed. That's the way deals with the police always work: one side adds a few extra terms to the deal, and the other side never knows it.

"Okay. She told me that he beat her, even in front of the children. That the Savasta family couldn't stand him and considered him half a man. Concerning last year's shooting, she made an allusion that as far as I'm concerned was unmistakable: Tempesta ordered his soldiers to injure the man."

"To warn him about what?"

"About minding his manners."

"So then he lost his temper, and nutcase that he is, he decided to punish his wife and his father-in-law by hiding the children," Gualtieri mused aloud.

Then he dismissed me by calling his secretary on the phone. He asked him to put a call through to the magistrate who had issued a warrant for the arrest. My time had expired; I could go back to the newspaper now and write my article.

Three hours later, the first copies were coming hot off the press, in the basement of our downtown office building. Banner headline: "Arrested for Kidnapping His Own Children." Subhead: "The suspect is Vito Carriglio, son-in-law of Mafia boss Tempesta. He refuses to say where he's hiding the children." Under that was my byline.

The editor in chief summoned me to his office, together with my news editor, to congratulate me. That had never happened before. I felt the urge to call my father, tell my mother, and hug Serena. Perhaps not in that exact order.

I went home after a second visit to police headquarters, in the hope that something else might leak out about the arrestee, Vito Carriglio. No one knew anything more than what I'd written in the article. I opened the apartment door just in time to hear the phone ring and someone pick up.

"No, I think he's still at the paper."

"Fabri, I'm here."

"Ah, here he is, he just got in. I'll put him on."

He put one hand over the mouthpiece and said to me: "It's the switchboard."

"You need to get back here immediately, the boss wants you: Carriglio told the police that he killed his three children."

● ● ● ● ●

I hadn't taken off that pair of jeans and that shirt for almost fourteen hours. The newsroom was buzzing. My boss summoned me to his desk.

"I talked to Gualtieri half an hour ago. That nut Carriglio told the prosecuting magistrate that he murdered his children and buried them in the Ficuzza forest. He was laughing while he said it. The prosecuting magistrate immediately called Gualtieri, and, in the name of the agreement that you have with him, he called you and then me."

"Has anyone gone to Ficuzza?"

"I was waiting for you. Carriglio talked about an agritourism bed and breakfast a couple of miles from where Carabinieri Colonel lo Turco was killed. There's a farmhouse that belongs to the mayor of Corleone. The bodies are supposed to be buried between the B&B and the farmhouse. Gualtieri's on his way with floodlights, the engineering corps, and police dogs."

"I'll leave immediately."

"But don't take your Vespa. Call Filippo, we need photographs. Take his car."

Fifteen minutes later, Filippo Lombardo was waiting for me in front of my apartment building at the wheel of his white Fiat 127. He had his Nikon FM2 on a strap around his neck, and his other cameras in his bag. Thirty miles, in the cool darkness of an October evening, driving over the Madonie mountains, amid crags that could have been anywhere but Sicily; chestnut forests, deep dark valleys. And between the farmhouse and the agritourism bed and breakfast, an hour later, the blinding glare of floodlights.

The prosecuting magistrate had authorized Carriglio to be present at the excavation site. That was the first time I saw the man: he was sitting on a tree stump, handcuffed, between two penitentiary officers who had accompanied him in a paddy wagon from the Ucciardone prison to the place where he claimed to have buried the corpses of his children. Carriglio was smoking a cigarette, holding it between the forefinger and middle finger of his right hand. His left hand was practically pressed against his right hand by the handcuffs, in a strange position that might have seemed to be one of prayer. He was a corpulent man; the prison overalls stretched to contain his belly: he was sweating in spite of the chilly mountain air. We walked over to him. Filippo's flash went off. He looked up at us.

"Journalists! I need to talk to you guys!" he shouted. His face reminded me of nothing so much as the mascaron of the Mouth of Truth in Rome.

"Shut up, Carriglio," said the policeman on his right, jamming an elbow into his ribs. He went back to his cigarette, forgetting about us. Meanwhile, the men from the military engineering corps were digging where Carriglio had directed them. The floodlights were illuminating the space as if it were high noon.

Filippo and I took a stroll around the patch of land. Gualtieri was in a squad car, talking into a radio mike. He was reporting to the chief of police.

Three children murdered in Palermo was an unpleasant piece of news; we needed to treat it more delicately than the *usual* round of Mafia murders. What did Palermo have to do with a massacre of children? What did Palermo have to do with the madness of a single man? In Palermo, death had always been administered with precision, in massive but specific doses, with respect for the methods that Cosa Nostra demanded: submachine guns, car bombs, bodies dissolved in acid, .357 Magnum bullets to the back of the head were all fine, but improvisation was strictly forbidden. The case was a bafflement to the Mafia liturgy; it hadn't been taken into account. Neither had wildcat operations, hurtling pieces of out-of-control shrapnel. But the man sitting just a few yards away from us, in handcuffs, looked like a collection of shrapnel.

They dug all night, but they uncovered nothing. No dead bodies. The place was full of earthworms, moles, manna ash trees, but no murdered children. At dawn, exhausted, the men with shovels were told to stop digging. Carriglio was sent back to his cell. His confession had proved a falsehood. Filippo and I, reeling from the cold and exhaustion, started back to Palermo. I thought back to the wife's words: "My husband doesn't deserve the truth. The truth is for honest people. Someone who steals his children from behind your back is a dishonest coward." The false truth of Vito Carriglio, child murderer.

We went straight to the paper. I wrote my piece and by eleven that morning I was already home. When I came in, I found Serena eating breakfast. She gave me a loving look and kissed me on the cheek. I stank. I didn't even bother to apologize. I took a shower and slipped into bed. At five that afternoon I woke up with no idea where I was or, more important, what time it was—but now my mother would have recognized me, at least. And that was a welcome change.

The apartment was empty. I remembered that Fabrizio had said he was going to Rome that morning: he'd enrolled in a three-day corporate management course. A note from Serena, which I found on the kitchen table, told me that she'd be back that night. It ended with a request: "I need to see you: we have to talk about Sunday. The forecast is excellent. I want to go to the beach." Cicova meowed, perhaps sensing my state of mind: a mixture of lust and terror.

It was a Friday in mid-October. An excellent day to talk about going to the beach.

• • • • •

Carriglio sent word from his cell that he wanted to talk to the prosecuting magistrate again. He denied that he'd murdered his children. He said that he'd been in a state of confusion, that he'd simply wanted to scare his wife and the rest of the Savasta family. The prosecuting magistrate requested that security measures be reinforced. They couldn't run the risk of his committing suicide, at least not until he'd told them where he was keeping the children hidden.

On Saturday morning, Gualtieri gave me all the particulars, which I used in my article; I wanted to explain to the readers that Carriglio was a dangerously unstable man. Capable of anything.

I submitted my piece and turned my thoughts to the sights and smells of the sea in autumn. According to the forecast, the temperature would be eighty degrees, with plenty of sunshine: I had a Sunday with Serena awaiting me.

A friend of ours, Antonio, invited us to come stay in his parents' house on the water, at the tip of the cape on the Gulf of Capaci. It was a villa I knew very well, with a terrace overlooking the Isola delle Femmine, the barren mountain of Sferracavallo, the orange groves of the plain of Villagrazia. And especially the sea. A vast expanse of water: peaceful, turquoise. Looking out from that terrace, in summers gone by, in years past, we'd waited for dawns and dreamed of sunsets. We'd gone in search of our first kisses there, fourteen-year-olds with lots of experience with rock and roll but not much with sex. It was our age of innocence. We talked about love, politics, the future, the careers we wanted for ourselves, the year 2000, which would be just like the year 1000, with bands of distraught souls sailing over our cities in flying saucers, flagellating themselves in fear of the end of everything, the beginning of everything, accompanied by lights that we imagined as sabering lasers, filled with psychedelic colors. Our wild fantasies were given a boost by the clumps of Lebanese and Moroccan hash that circulated in those days, wrapped in squares of aluminum foil, only to be crumbled into shredded tobacco and then rolled into huge, virtuoso three-paper joints. And then we'd talk about rock bands with spectacular names: Free, Black Sabbath, Yes, Jefferson Airplane...those had been the platforms of our dreams. And that Sunday we'd be going back to Antonio's villa, to the terrace from which all our desires were first launched into the air.

My sister swung by to pick up me and Serena at ten on Sunday morning. Her red Citroën Dyane took an hour to cover the twenty miles to the villa. Antonio was already there with Peppino, a classmate of his who was trying to work as an architect even before getting his degree or a license, and with Maristella, a silent, Middle Eastern—looking young woman who had opened a children's bookshop, the first one in Palermo.

Peppino had a villa nearby. His father, a criminal law-yer with a local reputation, owned a Boston Whaler that he moored offshore.

"Come on, let's sail over to Isola delle Femmine," he sug-gested as soon as we got there. "Swimsuits on, and we can go."

Serena tried to catch my eye and made a face, dropping her straw bag on the floor.

"I'm tired, I didn't get much sleep last night. I'd prefer to stay here and soak up some sun on the terrace." Her eyes sought mine again. I looked away.

"What about you?" Peppino asked me.

"I don't know, I ought to read the papers."

"Come on, stay and keep me company," said Serena, who'd changed into a bikini in the meantime. She was wear-ing a cotton two-piece suit decorated with a pattern of small yellow flowers, with a top secured by a knot in the back and a bottom that rode low on her hips, held together with a pair of skimpy cords. In the sunshine her skin looked amber gold and perfectly complemented her dark hair.

"I think I'd better stay, Peppì: I'll just stay and keep her company."

I was tired, and the idea really did appeal to me. The four of them went off, talking about the panini and *sfincione* they were planning to pick up at the bakery. They'd be back in the afternoon.

Serena stretched out on a green beach towel, looking out toward the sea. From there, the gulf was a perfect curve, defined by the islet out in front of us and the horizon line. I lay down next to her, on another towel. Facedown, just like her. I felt the warmth of the sun relaxing the muscles in the small of my back: there was no way I could read a newspaper flat on my belly. Serena said nothing, as if she'd fallen asleep. But the one who fell asleep was me.

The touch of her hand caressing my shoulders woke me up.

"Journalist, you're getting sunburned."

I heard her voice and suddenly remembered where I was and what I was doing.

"*Grazie*, Sere, but there's no risk of sunburn. I have Sicilian skin."

I stretched lazily, turned over onto my back. She smiled at me. She was smearing a little cocoa butter onto her face.

"You were asleep for an hour."

"I really am tired; it's been a tremendous week, and you know it." I sucked in my abdominals, as if my belly had been swallowed by my chest cavity.

"I wonder what Fabrizio's doing," said Serena, setting down her bottle of tanning oil.

"He's studying, he's always studying."

"He was supposed to call this morning, there won't be anyone to answer the phone."

"Don't you have his number in Rome?"

"Yes, but I didn't want to call him at nine o'clock on a Sunday morning: it seemed unfair to wake him up."

I looked at her: Serena wasn't the kind to worry about what was fair or unfair, she was someone who liked to play games. Dangerous games.

I leafed through *Il Corriere della Sera*: I found its graphic design intimidating. Its headlines even more so. It reported events that seemed to come from a universe that was radically different from ours. It talked about Southeast Asia, a terrifying terrorist attack on the Americans in Lebanon, and Star Wars—the missile defense shield, not the movie.

Scientific discoveries. I was envious of a world that was exotic and at the same time normal, a world that seemed so far from Palermo.

"I'm hungry," said Serena.

"I'll go see what's in the fridge."

"It's unplugged. I looked while you were sleeping. There's a can of chickpeas and a can of tuna in the pantry."

My skin was on fire. Sleeping in the sun had burned me to a crisp.

"I'm going to go take a shower, then I'll make you the best salad to be found anywhere near the Gulf of Capaci."

"Hurry up," she said with a smile.

I stood up, and I saw out of the corner of my eye that she had lain down and was taking off her bikini top.

I found the guest bathroom, slipped off my Port Cros swimsuit, and stepped into the shower. The water was cool; the spray was gentle. I felt my body temperature return to a seasonal level.

A minute later I saw her. Serena slid open the glass door and slipped under the spray, pressing close to my body. She was nude. Her breasts pressed against my chest, and without a word, she turned around. Her buttocks brushed against my penis.

The water was pouring over us; I could feel my heart beat. She turned around and faced me again, opened her eyes, stared at me, and moved her mouth closer to mine, while her hands explored my back. Then I felt the water pour into my mouth and her kiss slip down to my beard. I couldn't control my erection: I tried, but I couldn't do it. Inside me, the usual neon sign was blinking: HOWEVER. The adversative conjunctive adverb that rang out like a passage from the Bible, that compendium of every good deed that man can perform here on earth. And, inexplicably, I wanted to perform a good deed: control my erection, wipe the slate clean, confine those few minutes to a dream that I'd lock up in a cupboard with all the other wonderfully forbidden things that life had in store for me. The HOWEVER cupboard already had one fine item enjoying pride of place: Serena nude next to me, our toes intertwining, our hands touching, the desire doing a little preliminary stretching. I felt like a fool. She confirmed that sensation with a glance.

"All right," she said as she left the shower.

Nothing more.

I made a bowl of salad as if I'd taken a shower alone.

That Sunday ended in the silence of sunset, with us sipping a Messina beer on the terrace as we listened to the others' stories about the Isola delle Femmine and the sea urchins that Peppino had gathered and pried open for everyone. That night on the way home, as we were about to go in the door, Serena gave me a light kiss on the lips, and I didn't try to dodge it.

"I love you," she told me.

So did I, really. I loved her. I loved Fabrizio. And all the love I felt for the world at large that night kept me awake, forcing me into sweat-drenched dreams: the cocaine eyes of Vito Carriglio as he shouted: "Journalists! I need to talk to you guys!"; the sensation of Serena's bottom brushing against me; the blinking neon sign reading HOWEVER.

$$\bullet \ \bullet \ \bullet \ \bullet \ \bullet$$

I now think back on all the nos I've given and received. I'm still in the black: there are more yeses than nos. It was my good luck to grow up without any particular privations, even if it's clear to me that defeats do more to make you grow than victories do.

At the end of the eighties, with a group of trusted friends, I tried playing Privations, a game described by an American minimalist in one of his books. We gathered in a circle, on a fashionable beach, and the one who was "it" first said: "I've never been to Australia." Whoever had been to Australia had to give him a five-hundred-lire coin: his take was minimal. The others, who were as deprived of that experience as the one who had spoken, were under no obligation to pay. After travel, the statements soon shifted to the areas of love affairs and sex: "I've never had sex in a public place"; five people paid up. "I've never had a homosexual experience"; only one paid up. "I've never cheated on my partner"; and there was a chill in the air. A friend of mine, who was playing with his girlfriend sitting beside him, thought it over briefly and then set down a five-hundred-lire coin on the blue beach towel that was serving as our green felt table. His girlfriend looked down at the coin, leapt to her feet, and strode off toward the water in tears. We never played that game again.

And yet privations remain one of the pillars of our emotional growth. It makes you feel heroic to tell yourself no, to say no to the pleasure you can glimpse in a smiling invitation, in a pair of lips brushing against yours, destined to be nothing more than a couple of lives brushing past each other. You grow, you suffer, as if life itself were a hairshirt to be donned and worn.

As I look back, I can't say how many of those nos did me good, and I'm not thinking only of the field trips from the routine of love; I'm also thinking about career choices, the fear of taking on the new, reaching for the better instead of settling for the good. Other people's rejections aren't up to us, but we can encourage them: it's our own structure of certainties that makes others tilt toward a no.

At age twenty-four this was all pure intuition, a skin-sense of loyalty to ourselves and to friendship. We didn't know what regret was. Now we do, and we can feel it burn. Knowing, more-over, that all the yeses of life are written in our eyes.

● ● ● ● ●

"City news?"

"Yes."

"I have some things to tell you about the *picciriddi fatti scomparsi*—the children that were disappeared."

The same voice, the same sound like a dried walnut.

"*Buon giorno*, I'm listening."

I grabbed a piece of paper covered with writing and turned it over: underneath was a black Bic ballpoint.

"You need to take notes."

"I'm taking notes."

"Good. Now then: the three *picciriddi*? Vito Carriglio disappeared them in Sant'Onofrio."

He pronounced the words clearly, and his accent became harder, even wrinklier.

I scribbled the words. My heart was racing.

"Can you tell me where Sant'Onofrio is?"

"Did you take that note?"

"Yes, but—"

Click.

I sat there, staring at the sheet of paper. Then I thought of a small town by that name, over near Altavilla Milicia. I knew someone who lived there. I picked up the phone book for the province of Palermo. Rallo, Raspano, Ravanusa...Ravanusa, Salvatore: Contrada Sant'Onofrio, phone number 26.06.01.

It was there.

A house, a field, a grave, a prison?

I went to my news editor and told him about the phone call. We decided not to call the chief of the mobile squad immediately: after all, he'd had me followed, so he could wait a little while to find out. I'd check things out on my own. First I needed to talk with Carriglio's lawyer. And pay a call on Rosaria Savasta.

I started at the hall of justice. By noon the day's hearings were already over, and Counselor Giovanni Gallina was one of the lucky ones that day. I found him at the bar, his black robe draped over his arm, kidding around with two other colleagues. I walked over and as I approached, I heard that they were talking appraisingly about a female clerk of the court.

"You ought to see the *minne* on her," Gallina was saying as he raised a Stagnitta-brand demitasse of espresso to his lips. The other two lawyers joined in with some bawdy mimicry, tracing double B-cups in the air. They stopped snickering when they saw that I was heading straight for them.

"Counselor Gallina, forgive me for intruding."

I introduced myself, and he knew who I was: he'd been reading my articles about his client. The other two lawyers made themselves scarce, claiming a sudden urgent need to get back to their hearings.

"*Prego*, tell me what I can do for you," said Gallina, checking to make sure his charcoal-gray jacket was buttoned properly. He'd taken on an alert and professional tone of voice, the tone of a man about to earn a retainer.

"I'd be interested in talking to your client Carriglio."

"So would everyone. You can't imagine how many journalists have called me. But he's in prison, at the Ucciardone. It's not that easy to get a permit for a visit in there..."

"Pass me off as your assistant: we can go together."

"Why should I do that?"

"Because I have a piece of information that no one else has."

Counselor Gallina leaned a foot closer. His breath smelled of coffee.

"And just what would this piece of information be?"

"I know a name that might mean something to your client."

"And what would that mean to me?"

"That depends. The name is Sant'Onofrio."

The lawyer furrowed his brow and expressed his doubts: "What the fuck is Sant'Onofrio?"

"A place."

"Never heard of it."

"Maybe Carriglio has: Why don't you ask him, and then we can talk later this afternoon."

We exchanged phone numbers and a handshake.

I went back out onto the street.

The Vespa was parked in front of the newspaper. I released, all at once, the tension that had been building up inside me as I shoved my foot down onto the kick-starter. The engine turned over instantly. I was heading for Acqua dei Corsari.

The little building on Via Ettore li Gotti was just as dreary as it had been the first time I met Rosaria Savasta. Someone must have dumped an animal carcass next to a pile of garbage as tall as a truck. You couldn't see the carcass, but you could smell it.

I rang the bell. I announced my name.

The door clicked open.

Rosaria Savasta was a dark patch in the dim light of the landing. She was waiting for me with one hand on the anodized railing.

"What is it?"

"I have something to ask you."

"Come in."

I entered. I heard sounds coming from the kitchen. I imagined the old crow moving pots and pans by pecking at them with her beak.

"What is it?" she asked again, pointing me to a chair.

"Have you ever heard of a place called Sant'Onofrio?"

She made the distinctive Sicilian sound for no, clucking her tongue against the front of the roof of her mouth. As she made that sound, she jutted her chin out and tipped her head back. I once read that there are only two peoples on earth who nod their head vertically to express the word "no": a nomad people of the Sahel and the Sicilians.

"But this Sant'Onofrio must mean something. I got this from the same person who called me the first time."

I didn't say anything more. First I wanted to find out if she knew anything. Then I'd report to the mobile squad.

"No, that stinking *fituso* of a husband of mine never talked to me about this Sant'Onofrio."

"I didn't see you the other night at Ficuzza. It was a good thing you didn't come."

"I was with my father."

I thought about what would have happened if the bodies of the three children really had been buried there, in the Ficuzza forest. The delirious face of Vito Carriglio resurfaced in my memory. I imagined the days and nights of that married couple, in bed, waking up in the morning, during their meals, while the children were suffering from colic. The normal everyday life of a Mafia couple—he's a two-bit *malacarne*; she's the daughter of a mob boss. A violent, out-of-control life, with three little children who thought they had a mother and a father like everybody else.

"And just what did Signor Savasta say to you?"

She looked me up and down. The outcome of that glance would determine the likelihood of my learning anything. She decided to trust me: I hadn't written anything the first time, and I wouldn't write anything the second time either.

"It doesn't matter what my father said to me, what matters is what I asked him for."

"And what was that?"

"Vendetta."

Rosaria stood up and went into the kitchen. The noise of the pots and pans stopped as the echo of that word reverberated in the room: *vendetta*.

She came back a couple of minutes later. She didn't offer me anything to eat: she'd just wanted to take a break from herself and her anger.

"Signora Rosaria, what do you really know?"

"That that piece of stinking *fetenzia* took my children. If he killed them, he'll have to die."

"But why would Vito do something so horrible, why would he kill any children, especially his own children?"

"To show his contempt for me, and to show his contempt for my father. That's the most important thing to him: his miserable determination to punish my family."

"What did you ever do to him?"

"Nothing. If anything, we made him part of a family with a powerful name."

"I don't understand."

"You're a journalist: you weren't born to understand. What quarter do you come from?"

"I'm from Via Notarbartolo."

"Then you can't understand a thing."

"Why don't you explain it to me?"

She looked at me the way you look at little children who ask questions about what heaven is like.

"He was a good-looking boy, Vito was. He was twenty years old, big and strong. I noticed him outside a bar, he was making everyone laugh, he drove a souped-up Fiat 500 Abarth, he was selling contraband cigarettes. I liked the way he talked with people. I was a seventeen-year-old *signorina*, the daughter of Don Peppino Savasta. I was supposed to get married to someone on our same level. But that boy attracted me. I started to say *buon giorno* to him as I went past the bar. And he paid me compliments. We'd sneak out together for a gelato, or sandwiches with chickpea fritters. Two months later we eloped. We organized it carefully: he took a hotel room in Cefalù, I gave him my virginity, my youth, and once I'd been shamed—*svergognata*—then the only remedy was to get married."

I felt a certain degree of respect for this woman who had decided to tell the truth. She adjusted her hair, pulled back in a bun, and went on with her story.

"My father was helpless to do anything about it. Love had carried the day, or at least that's what I thought. The first child came immediately, a boy, Giuseppe, like his grandfather. Then Salvatore and finally Costanza. In the meantime Vito discovered what it meant to be part of a real family. Strict rules. No fooling around. Seriousness, utter respect. But he wasn't cut out for it. He was too *mafallannu* for my father, too much of a *useless thing*. And he could sense how my family looked down their noses at him. He started to make excuses every time there was an official holiday that involved a family meal. He'd say that he had to pick up a load of cigarettes, or else that he had a little job to do at Arenella. He just didn't want to see my family. He didn't want to sense the condemnation he could see in their eyes. He spent as little time at home as possible; I raised the children myself, with the help of my sister Assunta, who remained unmarried, still Signorina Assunta."

I took mental notes. A mountain of information that might well prove useful.

"When did the drugs start?"

"Two, three years ago. Cocaine. Vito changed from one day to the next. He went crazy. He always seemed to have a fever, his eyes bugging out, watery. He raised his hands to me every day: a slap, a kick, no matter what I said. I threatened to tell my father. Then he'd stop, but after thinking it over he'd slap me again, or punch me. He hated my father and I was a part of my father. He raised his hands to me in front of my children…"

"Yes, you told me about that."

"So I threw him out. He found a place to live, I don't know where, and he took the children to sleep at his sister's place, in Passo di Rigano. And then they never came back."

She fell silent.

Her eyes were still dry. That woman was a piece of tufa stone, a hewn block you could build a cathedral with.

"What did your father say when you asked him to take vengeance?"

"He's my father: What do you think he said?"

She got to her feet. I heard the gong ring. Round over.

Rosaria Savasta saw me to the door, and, as I was walking down the first flight of stairs, she said: "The truth...Vito Carriglio doesn't deserve the truth. I want you to remember that."

Via Ettore li Gotti welcomed me back, with its stench of a rotting carcass. My ten-year-old Vespa was the newest thing for a mile around.

• • • • •

On my way home I summed up the content of that conversation: Vito Carriglio was practically a dead man walking.

The October afternoon cooled off, and the khaki fatigue jacket was light for the brisk sea breeze I could feel hitting me as I sped down Via Messina Marine on my Vespa. The Cala harbor was illuminated, and the moored sailboats were rocking gently. On the waterfront boardwalk, the best focaccia shop of Mandamento Tribunali was lit by a five-hundred-watt fishing lamp, which hung over the cauldron where the spleen was bubbling in the hot lard. Out of the corner of my eye, I saw two men, holding a little boy by one hand each, bite into those focaccias. I smiled at the thought of that Palermitan aperitif.

When I got home, Fabrizio was there. The sound of a piano came from the living room. Delicate, harmonious notes, in sharp contrast with the day I'd had.

"Fabri, what are you listening to?"

"Serena put it on. Erik Satie."

I went to take a look at the album cover: *Gymnopédie*.

"Sere is in the bathroom, she's taking a shower. I'm going to play some soccer. I'll be back by eleven, and if you want we can go over to Ilardo's to get a gelato."

"Fine. We'll have something to eat and wait for you."

A plan that involved a crime. Or at least the willingness to commit one.

Fabrizio picked up his gym bag and left. Serena was still in the bathroom.

Cicova looked up at me imploringly. He followed me into the kitchen and I opened a can of tuna and rice for him. I cleaned the kitty litter and changed the water in his bowl. He was the only creature I could trust at that moment: he deserved good treatment.

I treated Serena well, too, when I saw her walk in wrapped in Fabrizio's bathrobe, with a towel twisted atop her head, a turban for her wet hair.

"I made you a cocktail: white wine and crème de cassis. The stupidest drink there is, they call it a Kir. You want it?"

"Certainly I want it, journalist."

She gave me a damp kiss on my beard. I smelled the scent of shower soap and shampoo wafting into the air from her warm body. A sweet sensation.

"What did you do today, Sere?"

"Seventeenth-century art, there's no getting away from it."

"Didn't you go out?"

"Your friend and I went to Piazza Marina to see Palazzo Steri. He told me that in the seventeenth century, in that palazzo, the Inquisition had its headquarters, and they burned people at the stake right out front, where the giant magnolia fig trees are now."

"Did you see the cells?"

"No."

"There are still words carved into the walls by miserable wretches who were about to be burned at the stake."

"I have to say that you Palermitans—"

"That those Roman Catholics, I think you should say…"

"Sure, but all the same, death is a constant theme in your minds."

"Just a short walk from the Steri there's a painting that represents us perfectly: it's called *The Triumph of Death*; I don't know if Fabrizio took you to see it."

"That's a pleasure we're saving for our golden years."

She laughed. I drank up the last of my Kir.

"What do you want to eat?" I asked her.

"Whatever there is."

I opened the refrigerator. I saw some red tomatoes.

"I could make some pasta with a *picchio-pacchio* sauce."

"I'll trust you."

"Tomatoes sautéed in a garlic and oil base."

"I'll trust you even more."

She went to change.

Twenty minutes later we were sitting down to dinner.

For dinner, I'd put on the Velvet Underground with Nico. She wasn't even willing to wait for "Femme Fatale" to come on before she started talking about what had happened between the two of us at Antonio's villa.

"You're an unusual person," she said without glancing at me.

"Why?"

"Other guys wouldn't have stopped."

"I never got started."

She shot me a cold, hard glare. Then she took another forkful of spaghetti.

"Okay. You and your friends…" She shook her head. "What the fuck, you Palermitans."

"I really care about Fabrizio. He's my better half."

She laughed: "No, he's mine."

She'd laughed it off, and I was happy she had.

"You know how much it cost me not to get started?"

Her gaze softened. Everybody likes a compliment.

Cicova leapt onto my legs, rubbing his head against the edge of the table. Then he stretched out, as if he'd fainted. I scratched his belly: as I touched him I understood the meaning of the word "ecstasy."

Serena cleared the table. When she picked up my plate, she caressed my beard. I also understood the meaning of the word "terror." I feared that the strength I'd displayed at the villa might abandon me unexpectedly.

She went into the kitchen and cleaned up all by herself. I took the Velvet Underground off and turned on the TV. We sat at an amiable distance watching a French movie that was playing on a private network: the story of a television repairman falling for his first love all over again, and then another guy who was head over heels in love shows up and gets down on one knee and declares his love for her. In other words, a movie about love.

At eleven o'clock we heard the door open. Fabrizio threw his gym bag on the floor and called us: "You guys ready?"

The *pezzi duri* that Ilardo made took us into territory that we'd already explored and was therefore safe: I ordered chocolate, Serena ordered Chantilly rice, and Fabrizio ordered cassata. We were a family, a bit Jules and Jim and a bit otherwise, but whatever—it was all fine.

Before falling asleep I thought once again about Vito Carriglio and Rosaria Savasta. What love could there have been between the two of them? What misunderstandings could have generated that physical attraction? How important had whatever affinities might have existed been? How crucial is the idea of being kindred spirits, twin souls? I saw Fabrizio's and Serena's hands, intertwined in the darkness of the room. Then I saw my hands and Serena's. In another world, possibly.

I fell asleep with a picture in my mind: her white knuckles, her long, tapered fingers wrapped in mine.

• • • • •

The telephone rang at seven in the morning. I managed to answer before it woke up Fabrizio and Serena: there are certain sounds that fit right into a dream, and I hoped that was the case for them.

"This is Counselor Gallina."

"*Buon giorno*, counselor."

"Last night I talked to my client, at the Ucciardone prison. He was pretty down. I told him about Sant'Onofrio and his face lit up. He asked me who knew about that place. I mentioned your name. I explained that you're a journalist. He turned gloomy again. He said nothing for a while. Then he told me: All right, I want to talk to this journalist."

"Today?"

"This morning, if that's all right with you."

"I'm ready."

"I'll tell them that you're my paralegal. They don't know you at the prison, right?"

"That's right."

"Well then, at eleven o'clock, in front of the loading dock on Via Enrico Albanese."

"At eleven it is."

I swung by the paper and notified my boss of the appointment to visit the prison. I told him to set aside plenty of

space: I was sure this was going to be a scoop. After the meeting in the prison, I'd alert the head of the mobile squad. I read
the morning papers absentmindedly and sat out the planning
of the day's issue: all I could think about was Vito Carriglio's
sweaty face that night in the Ficuzza forest, his cocaine eyes,
and the words he'd shouted: "Journalists! I need to talk to you
guys!" I jotted down the mental notes I'd taken during my
conversation with Rosaria Savasta. I built up a small outline
on the sheet of paper:

Motive: Vito's anger.

Target: her family.

Weapon: the three children.

I reread that last line: I felt a wave of shame. For myself
and for him. How can three innocent lives become the tools
of a vendetta?

I crumpled up the sheet of paper and tossed it in the trash.

I went back to my notes about Rosaria, that proclama-
tion of hers: "Vito Carriglio doesn't deserve the truth." It was
probably a fair statement, but her children did. The truth was
waiting for me in the Ucciardone prison visiting room, and
I'd be there in two hours.

• • • • •

I parked my Vespa on the sidewalk, on Via Enrico Albanese.
The prison guards watched the process with an air of indif-
ference. I stood close to the prison wall near the guards'
booth and waited for Counselor Gallina. I'd brought a leather
briefcase that I'd borrowed from a fellow journalist, hoping to
make myself look professional.

"What's in the bag?" the lawyer asked as he approached
with an indolent swagger.

I opened the briefcase and found a copy of Dostoevsky's *White Nights and Other Stories*, the September issue of *Quaderni Piacentini*, a Diabolik comic book, a ChapStick, and an eyeglass case.

"Can I take it in with me?"

"It doesn't look like the kinds of things a lawyer would carry. If they ask to look inside, tell them that only the Diabolik is yours. Everything else belongs to your girlfriend. Trust me."

I nodded. He handed over his bar association membership card, and I gave them my identity document; on the line for occupation, it said "office worker." A little trick that a veteran reporter on the courts beat had taught me when I first started working on the city news desk: "Make sure to get a new piece of ID that doesn't identify you as a journalist. It's always a good idea not to tell the truth. Go down to city hall and make sure they put down that you're an office worker, just to keep from scaring anyone." He was a good journalist, a member of a venerable old profession. The proof of the technique's effectiveness was in the eyes of the prison guard as he studied my ID. He nodded to his colleague, and the door loudly clicked open.

"Let in the lawyer and his assistant."

I'd never been to the Ucciardone prison before. I hoped never to enter through the other door, the one for prisoners and suspects. The courtyard was a shadowy gray, faced in smooth stone. The star-shaped plan had been designed by the architect Nicolò Puglia, at the behest of King Ferdinand I, at the turn of the nineteenth century. Each wing of the prison was a circle out of Dante's Inferno, under the control of the Mafia.

Vito Carriglio was in one of the wings reserved for ordinary criminals. He hadn't even been considered worthy of *picciotto* status. Crimes against children, back then, were viewed with disdain even by Cosa Nostra.

The guards led us to Wing 3, North Side. We climbed stairs. Through the barred windows that provided some light to the hallway we could glimpse Monte Pellegrino. I saw Castello Utveggio, its red stone touched by the fingers of the morning sun. The view was not one suggestive of incarceration, at least if you looked out the window. The lawyer directed me to a solid hardwood door at the end of the corridor: the entrance to the visiting room of Wing 3. The guards let us in and then went away, locking the door behind them. In the room there was a table bolted to the floor; around it stood four Formica chairs. We sat down.

The silence of the room was immediately shattered by the creak of the opening door. Two prison guards came in, followed by a corpulent man in a blue tracksuit, with shackles and chains on his wrists. I recognized the feverish eyes, now devoid of any trace of defiance. He looked like a sick man.

"Carriglio, we're going to chain one hand to this table. Remember, behave, or in we come. Counselor..." concluded the first guard, touching the visor of his cap in a gesture of respect.

"*Grazie*," Gallina replied.

The two officers left the room.

Vito Carriglio met my gaze: he hadn't recognized me, but he knew that he'd be talking to the man who had mentioned Sant'Onofrio, and now he also knew that that man was me.

"Counselor, *chistu cu è?*" he asked all the same.

"The journalist, the one who knows things."

"And what do you know, *vossia?*" he asked me, using the Sicilian term of address.

"I know that your *picciriddi* are at Sant'Onofrio. But you need to help us: tell us where and how to find them."

Vito Carriglio gazed at me as if I were a landscape rather than a human being. His eyes wandered to some random point just above the top of my head. Then, with his free hand, he covered his eyes and sat silently.

"I'm not crazy," he began, in the tone of voice of someone trying to explain. "I hate the Savasta family, I hate my wife and all her people. They've treated me as if I were less than nothing. Maybe I am, you're a journalist and you know what less than nothing amounts to, you've studied, you see people, you understand everything."

I thought of his wife's words, when she'd told me that I couldn't understand a thing. I nodded my head in agreement; I didn't want to interrupt.

"You must have understood that I had no choice in this. I had to punish my wife and all her people. They don't feel pain. You can sting them and they just laugh. But there is one thing they care about: the family. The blood family. The children, the children's children…and I hated them with a hatred that was stronger than the love that I have for my children."

The love that I have.

"So they're still alive?"

"Let me go on. *Vossia* needs to keep quiet. I've decided to tell the truth and I have to explain it my way."

"Forgive me."

Counselor Gallina touched my leg.

"Friday at noon I went to get them in my Fiat 128, the way I do every week. Giuseppe sat in the front seat, and Salvatore and Costanza sat in back. They asked me: Papà, what, are we going to stay with our aunt? No, I told them, no we're not. This time we're going to the country. There's a surprise. And I drove toward the highway, Statale 113, Ficarazzi, Bagheria, Solanto, Altavilla Milicia. We got to Contrada Sant'Onofrio before the clock struck one. I was taking them to a farmhouse I had rented—you don't say a word, I won't say a word—a few months back. Three rooms, middle of the olive groves. Before going to the farmhouse we went through the town of Altavilla: I wanted to buy some mulberries. Costanza's crazy about them and they're about to go out of season. I stopped in the middle of the road; there was an old man with a wicker basket full to overflowing with mulberries: sweet, delicious, *tardoni*—end of the season. I paid him for a kilo, and then we went to the house. In the trunk of the Fiat 128, I had a bag of fava beans and a big roll of duct tape. I let the kids out and they started playing in the yard with the *strummula*, you know, a spinning top, what do you all call it? I told them to stay home and be good because I had to go to town and buy a few more things. Half an hour later I came back with two tanks of propane. We spent a very nice afternoon, the three of them napping as I shelled the fava beans, making dinner. It was a pretty evening; I waited for nightfall before sitting down to dinner: fava bean soup, bread, and mulberries for dessert. The three of them were famished, they kept saying: Papà, what time is dinner? And I said: now, now, dinner's ready. In the kitchen

I poured a bottle of sleeping pills into the soup, I think the brand name was Minias. The way they gobbled down that soup was a pleasure to see. Then the mulberries. Costanza gave me a kiss, Giuseppe and Salvatore were tired: they were both yawning. Or it might have been the sleeping pills...in ten minutes they were asleep on the sofa, like a pile of puppies, the two boys holding hands. I carried two mattresses into the living room. I took the duct tape and started sealing all the windows. I laid the three of them out on the mattresses. By the time I was done working it was ten o'clock. Then I carried the two propane tanks into the living room, opened both of them, and went out into the yard. The sky was covered with stars. I looked up: it was beautiful."

My heart was about to stop.

"I'll even tell you where my children are: the tenth olive tree on the right, looking out from the house. I made sure they were clean and tidy before I put them in the grave, I dressed them nicely, and I wiped off the foam they had on their mouths."

I was unable to speak. I touched Counselor Gallina's arm. His eyes had filled with tears. He lifted his hand and touched me back, lightly, a brotherly pat: solidarity between survivors of a shipwreck. We were eyewitnesses to horror; the meaning of life was drowning before our eyes. We sat for two minutes in silence in that room where the table was bolted to the floor. There was nothing left to say. Actually, we were bolted to the spot: to reality, to hatred.

Vito Carriglio's expression hadn't changed a bit; he looked at his defense lawyer and asked him for a cigarette.

• • • • •

An hour later, a dozen squad cars were on their way to Contrada Sant'Onofrio, in search of the tenth olive tree, the olive tree of horror. The engineering corps showed up with shovels and floodlights.

A crowd of townspeople gathered: word had spread rapidly. I was with Filippo Lombardo, who was photographing everything in sight: the little house, the olive grove, the squad cars with their flashing lights, the beginning of the excavations.

I was sitting off to the side, on a bench in front of the house where, probably, that Friday afternoon, the children had tied strings to their *strummule* and spun them. I was looking out at some random point in the countryside, as if in search of consolation. In the distance, I heard the screams of Rosaria Savasta. Darkness fell. An old man with a gray cap and a brown fustian suit sat down next to me. He asked me for a cigarette. I gave him one. Then he said: "Do you work for the city newsroom?"

City newsroom? That voice, that tone, like a dried walnut. "Yes, I work the city beat. Then you..."

"In that case you must be the journalist I called. I had a suspicion: you were the first one to show up this afternoon."

"But what did you know?"

"Nothing. That a car had come into town and that there was a man, a *cristiano*, driving, and three little ones, *tre picciriddi*. They asked me for a kilo of mulberries and I sold it to them. Then, the next day, I saw the same car drive off, with only the *cristiano* at the wheel. I asked around. Who he was, who he wasn't. I found out the name. To me, this story of children who were in the car and then children who weren't there anymore, it didn't sit well. It made me think. And I had to tell someone about it."

"*Grazie.*"

"*Di niente,*" the man said. "Don't mention it."

He stood up and walked past the floodlights: his dark suit swallowed the light.

Nothing and no one glittered that night.

ROSALIA
A Daughter

MILAN, JANUARY 2011

The dark eyes of a girl who wanted certainties staring into mine, brimming over with angry tears. I have a clear memory of that meeting. The wound left by Palermo was deep in her. She was asking me to help her find her way back to a future that her circumstances were denying her. I was just a journalist doing his best to separate himself from his work. Over here, the young man; over there, the beat reporter. It was the only way to keep from being overwhelmed by the death-dealing stench of blood. In those years, Cosa Nostra had lost its mind. It was reacting in a ferocious, disproportionate manner, chasing after a dream of power straight out of Shakespeare: in order to force the world to kneel at its feet, it was willing to forget there had ever been rules. So the Mafia broke solemn promises bosses had made to one another, cruelly persecuted the weak, dissolved children in baths of acid, slaughtered women, mutilated corpses.

Deep in every Sicilian's heart, there is an icy madness.

PALERMO, FEBRUARY 1984

"*Dottore*, you need to come see this. Over."

"Vela 2, what is it?"

"A 10-79. It's absurd. Over."

"Give me the location."

"Piazza Giulio Cesare. Over."

"Sorry, but Vela 2, where's that?"

"*Dottore*, come on, the train station. Over."

The guy who covered the political beat, Pippo Suraci, looked up from his Olympia typewriter, stopped pounding the keys, and, speaking to no one in particular, said: "I wonder what happened at the station?" Then he went back to writing.

The news editor lit an MS cigarette and waved me over with his lighter. I stepped closer. I'd heard the police radio, too. A 10-79 was code for a request for a medical examiner: a murder had been committed. And an "absurd" one, too, according to what the officer on the scene had just said.

My boss waved his lighter, pointing to the door of the newsroom. His lips were inhaling smoke. He didn't even have time to say: "Go."

"Okay, I'm going. I've got a pocketful of phone tokens, and if I find a working phone I'll let you know."

"The train station is the only place in Palermo where you can find working phone booths. As soon as you get there, give me a call, because we're about to put the paper to bed. And take a photographer with you," my boss said, chewing on the smoke.

I called up to the photographers' room. Filippo Lombardo answered and a few seconds later he was downstairs at the front desk of the building. I told him to hop on the back of my Vespa, and in eight minutes flat we were at Piazza Giulio Cesare: I'd never known that was the name of the piazza in front of the train station.

"Be a beat reporter, you'll learn all about the world," my first editor in chief had told me. And now I was learning.

Three squad cars with their flashing blue lights, a dozen policemen, an ambulance: all of them clustering around a gray Ford Escort abandoned in the middle of the piazza, theoretically double parked. I spotted the *"dottore,"* Antonio Gualtieri. Even the chief of the mobile squad had come out to see.

We exchanged a quick greeting. Filippo mounted his flash-gun. It was noon on a winter day: the gray sky cast a flat, ugly light on the scene. The piazza was the usual picture of chaos: a group of taxis; three horse-drawn carriages, their drivers wielding whips; cars parked like so many pickup sticks. A wave of humanity that washed into and out of one of the farthest-flung train stations on the entire Italian peninsula. I knew that piazza: every trip I took back then was by train and followed the rule of "plus fourteen." Paris? Eighteen hours from Rome, plus fourteen more to reach Rome from Palermo. Amsterdam? Twenty hours, plus fourteen. I saw lots of Europe, I met plenty of people: it wasn't a geographic handicap, it was just the distance necessary to understand the journey.

"What's happened, Antonio?"

"Come and see for yourself."

Filippo was behind me, and he test-fired his flashgun. Gualtieri opened the passenger door of the Ford Escort. There was something the size of a soccer ball on the front seat, concealed under a newspaper.

Gualtieri lifted the paper and two eyes, a nose, and a mouth appeared, the color of antiqued leather. The effect was straight out of Madame Tussaud's, but both Gualtieri and I knew very well that wax had never been popular in Palermo. The city had always preferred lead.

The man's head was sitting on the practically brand-new fabric upholstery of the Ford Escort's passenger seat. There wasn't a drop of blood anywhere around it. The eyes were closed, the mouth pursed in a whisper, the hair tousled but nicely arranged around a face that looked to be about forty. That head would gladly have spoken. Perhaps words of love, or else a curse.

I noticed how Filippo's flashgun lit up the car's interior. Then Gualtieri led me around to the rear of the Escort.

"Cucuzza, open the trunk."

The officer obeyed. In the trunk was a well-dressed corpse: a dark-brown three-piece suit, black shoes, a shirt that must have once been white. The tie lay beside the body, since the neck around which it had once been knotted was no longer there. The corpse had been arranged to fit in that tiny space: the Ford Escort had won the title of "Car of the Year" for 1981, but it was still a compact sedan. There was not a trace of blood in the trunk, either.

"Antonio, what ideas have you come up with?" I asked Gualtieri.

"Must have been Robespierre," he said with a laugh, and I joined in to jolly him along.

"I don't remember any beheadings in Palermo," I said. I'd been working the crime beat for almost five years, so I considered myself a veteran.

The chief of the mobile squad looked at me the way you look at an abstract painting: with interest, but with some misgivings about the artist's ability.

"We don't even know what his name is. Before we talk about precedents, we ought to identify him."

"I'll come by your office later on."

"All right."

The only reason he agreed was that he knew my father was a Juventus fan—a Juventino—in addition to rooting for Palermo. When I told him that, the first time he agreed to see me, I made him happy. He immediately trotted out the collection of pennants that Giampiero Boniperti had given him when he was a young officer working the Turin stadium. Half the population of Palermo, by tradition, rooted for Juve as their second team. This was the legacy of a mysterious culture that long ago drove Sicilian pastry chefs, descendants of the geniuses who invented the *cassata* in the tenth century, to create a chocolate cake that's better than the Austrian Sacher torte and call it the "*torta Savoia.*" A Savoy torte in Palermo. A form of *contrappasso*, like Dante's poetic justice, but gastronomic in nature: much as if the Milanese, instead of inventing their renowned cutlet, had invented *michette con il kebab*.

I went back to the paper. I reported to my news editor, who still had time to do a new layout of the front page. Filippo handed over the photograph, still wet with developer and stop bath. A photograph perfectly poised between the Middle

Ages and the late twentieth century, worthy of a latter-day Bosch: a man's head, perfectly bloodless, sitting on a black-and-white checkered car seat, surrounded by dashboard, stick shift, steering wheel; the interior of an automobile, the exterior of a nightmare. Above the full-page photograph, a banner headline screamed: "The Mystery of the Severed Head."

Half an hour later, the newsies invaded the city waving copies of the paper, fresh from the press, as they shouted the lullaby of Palermo: *"How many died, how many died."*

• • • • •

At the medical examiner's office, the two parts of the body were temporarily reassembled. Dr. Filiberto Quasazza, head of the office, authorized an autopsy and a series of photographs of the head. They were able to ascertain that the man had been strangled to death and then decapitated. The tool used to remove the head had been as sharp as a guillotine, whatever it was. Dr. Quasazza's assistants joked as they stood around the marble autopsy table, the most educated of the group making references to the Terror and wondering if "terrorists" were therefore followers of the French revolutionaries. The pictures taken in the morgue were then sent immediately to police headquarters.

After looking through a thousand or so mug shots, at six that evening, Gualtieri's mobile squad ascertained that the head had once belonged to Giovanni Neglia, born in Porticello on March 5, 1934, with previous convictions for theft.

"Dottore, we've got a name," said Inspector Zoller, setting down a typed sheet of paper on the desk of the chief of the mobile squad.

I had just walked into the office a few minutes earlier.

"*Buona sera*, Inspector," I said, getting to my feet.

"Good work, boys: you were quick," Gualtieri commented.

"It's all written down here, you only need to read it," Zoller added, pointing to the sheet of paper. With every word, his salt-and-pepper mustache rose and fell, as if in a children's cartoon.

Gualtieri waved him out with a smile.

"Antonio, who does that head belong to?" I asked.

"Let me see…Neglia. Giovanni Neglia. A two-bit thief."

"Do you know what *neglia*, or really *negghia*, means in the Palermo dialect?"

"No."

"A good-for-nothing, an incompetent," I explained.

"Too bad for him."

"What else does it say?"

"Previous convictions, born in Porticello in 1934, married, father of two daughters."

"Would you give me the address?"

"Via Perpignano 36. His wife is named Cosima."

At the door on my way out, Gualtieri made the sign of the horns with his fingers to ward off bad luck, slapped me on the back, and practically shoved me out of his office.

Tomorrow I'd start work on the severed head of Signor Good-for-Nothing.

● ● ● ● ●

"Venditti is whiny," said Serena.

"No, he's romantic," Lilli replied.

"All romantics are whiny."

"Oh, you're horrible."

"And you're a romantic."

As I walked into the apartment, I happened to pick up this fragment of conversation. Serena hated anything that smacked of sugar, while Lilli was as sweet as, say, Antonello Venditti's hit *"Le tue mani su di me."* Perhaps I was starting to fall in love with her. I loved her blonde hair, the look in her eyes that reminded me of the Sicilian sea. Her soft, yielding hips. The simple love that she had for being in love: she'd cuddle next to me at night and watch the stupidest programs on TV; she'd lavish me with compliments, whatever I cooked for her; she wanted me to read poems aloud. And she was completely unrestrained in her lovemaking. Lilli was twenty-two years old and was enrolled in college majoring in literature, but she'd never even taken a final exam, much less flunked one. Her father, a very well-to-do commercial accountant, heir to a Palermitan family with only one-quarter nobility—and of Bourbon descent, to make things worse—had set her up with her own little toy store to run. We'd met at a New Year's party thrown by my sister. She'd shown up with her boyfriend, a tall guy with a mélange wool turtleneck. I decided that one thing you should never do is welcome in the New Year with an indecisive color: it shows a lack of respect for the future. I ignored him and went over to my sister, who was greeting the blonde girl who had come to the party with the mélange turtleneck.

"This is Lilli."

She was wearing a skintight dress that allowed me to admire her curves, which were described in great detail by the charcoal-gray fabric of her dress. She had a warm beauty that occupied a perfect middle ground between Sicily's Norman DNA and its Phoenician ancestry. She turned to look at me and immersed her blue eyes in mine, scalding them until they were fully cooked, a couple of pan-fried eggs, over easy. I took her left hand delicately and held it in mine, without a word. The strangeness of that gesture forced her to take another look at me. I returned her gaze without flinching, and with a smile I told her who I was and what I did, without ever releasing her hand, which I could feel growing warmer. Her hand didn't shake mine off; it curled up in my palm, or at least that's what I thought. I found out I'd been right at three that morning, when I suggested we abandon the mélange turtleneck to its fate. She accepted. Later, at the apartment, we'd talk about our lives, kneading them together like so much dough.

"Okay, girls. Just don't fight over the music, please."

"I never fight," said Serena, glaring daggers at me.

"*Ciao, amore mio.*" Lilli kissed me softly on the lips.

"Where's Fabrizio?" I asked.

"He's on his way, he had a lesson," Serena replied.

I looked at the clock. It was eight.

"Shall we go out when he gets here?"

The two young women exchanged a glance filled with questions. Cold out? Tired? How to get there? Take Fabri's Renault 4? And what would they eat?

Lilli said: "You decide."

Serena corrected her: "No. I couldn't say, let's wait for Fabrizio."

Cicova had listened to the conversation curled up on the sofa. Now and then he opened an eye. He stretched out and enjoyed the first few notes of "In a Sentimental Mood." He arched his back and yawned. Then he came toward me, with a rolling gait.

"I'll cook dinner for everyone: for you girls, for Fabri when he gets home, for Cicova. Come on, kitties, come with me to the kitchen," I said, addressing Lilli and Serena. Serena showed me her middle finger, with a verbal garnish: "Go fuck yourself, journalist."

I explored the refrigerator and the pantry. What I came up with was an eggplant, two zucchinis, a carrot, some onions, a head of garlic, some dried red peppers, a bunch of withered basil, and two pounds of D'Amato spaghetti, from Porticello.

Porticello. Giovanni Neglia. The decapitated thief.

I suppressed the thought and went in search of a cutting board: the ingredients would have to be diced and then sautéed in a pan, garlic and onions first, until the whole thing had cooked down to a wonderful vegetable-and-herb topping. I called it "spaghetti *alla* everything."

Fabrizio came in as I was draining the pasta. He said: "*Ciao.*" Then he asked: "Who the fuck put Coltrane on the stereo? I'm in a bad mood, and tonight I just want to listen to Venditti." Serena rolled her eyes. Lilli stifled a laugh. I took the blame for Coltrane, without explaining that it had been put on as a peacemaking gesture. I decided to gloss over the details.

The spaghetti was excellent. Lilli suggested we go to Villa Sperlinga and get a round of *spongati.* Fabri offered to drive. We were all in our twenties: a gelato with your friends, with your lovers, in your favorite café, was still the best thing imaginable. And a metal cup of *spongato* at Villa Sperlinga was the best gelato this world offered.

• • • • •

A few months earlier, a Carabinieri captain I was about to make friends with was murdered. The Cosa Nostra killers who did him in shot him in his squad car. While they were at it, they killed the other two carabinieri who were riding with him. His name was Mario D'Aleo, he was from Rome, and he was twenty-nine years old. We'd met frequently, at the scenes of other murders, and we'd talked about everything imaginable. He looked like a typical carabiniere, with a mustache that made him look like the actor Maurizio Merli, only dark-haired. He was a handsome young man, with the interests and curiosities of our generation. He'd replaced another captain of the Carabinieri murdered by the Mafia a few years before that.

I remember that, as usual, a preliminary, fragmentary report had come in to the newspaper: a triple murder on Via Scobar. I went with a photographer and a television cameraman, and along the way we'd discussed whether the victims were more likely to be from "their side" or "our side." The furious rage that surrounded us when we got there answered our question. Clearly, they'd killed someone from "our side." I remember standing there, tears streaming from my eyes, as I looked at that car with CARABINIERI written on the sides: I recognized Mario D'Aleo and all the marks of injustice.

There was nothing remarkable about it: those were times when people died. We had no other form of defense than to find a snug little corner somewhere to hide from reality. My sheltering burrow was the apartment I shared with Fabrizio, the sweet gaze in Lilli's eyes, stupid games, good music, a bowl of spaghetti. We had no self-awareness, no idea that we were fighting a war: we counted our dead; we felt Death's talons plunging a little deeper every day into our lives. I was in Palermo's relentless clutches; I was getting ready to start experimenting with psychopharmaceuticals in an attempt to treat the insomnia that was tormenting me at age twenty-five.

• • • • •

"Have you spoken to the family?"

"I'd like to go see them this morning."

"Then why are you still standing here?"

The news editor was scrutinizing me with the eyes of an entomologist. He was making me feel like an insect: not a very good feeling at 7:09 in the morning.

"I'm still here because I wanted you to tell me that I ought to go see the family."

"If you don't go see the family instantly, I swear I'll step on you and crush you."

There: an insect.

I grabbed my navy-blue blazer and a notepad and, as I was heading downstairs, tried to think of the shortest route to Via Perpignano. When I got to number 36, I found a wooden door and an intercom panel with six surnames written in ballpoint ink: "Neglia" was between "Adelfio" and "Pipitone." I rang the bell. Nothing happened. After a few seconds, a fat woman dressed in black wearing a checkered apron stuck her head out a third-story window. She was careful as she leaned out: it was more a French door than a window, and it opened onto thin air; there was no balcony railing.

"The doorbell is broken. But who is *vossia* looking for?"

"The Neglia family."

"And just who would you be?"

"A journal—"

She slammed the French door before I could finish. I rang the bell again. The fat woman appeared again.

"Now what are you doing? Do you want me to call the police?"

"The police told me to come here in the first place."

The woman didn't know what to say. She understood that she needed to be careful: she probably started wondering just who I really was. A customary question in Sicily.

"All right. Third floor."

The whole place smelled of *sparacelli*, a particular type of broccoli, tender, bright green. You have to boil *sparacelli* from morning to night to get the proper consistency.

The woman took off her apron and waved me to a chair. The table was covered by a flowered plastic tablecloth. The scent of *sparacelli* came wafting powerfully out of the nearby kitchen.

"Are you Signora Cosima?"

Silence rang out, providing all the answer I needed.

"Please accept my condolences."

She was squeezed into mourning black, a flannel dress. I heard sounds coming from another room nearby.

She murmured, "*Grazie*," then added: "They're going to let us see him today."

I certainly hoped they wouldn't.

"Signora Cosima, what kind of a person was your husband?"

"He was a good man, a good father, a wonderful husband."

"Would you happen to have a photograph?"

"*'Nca cierto.* Rosalia!"

The noise stopped. A girl appeared in the doorway. She looked like a young Claudia Cardinale, and she wore an unadorned black dress. Her hair was dark, her eyes were the color of pitch, and her face was oval, with a small nose and a full mouth with rosy lips and a pout on it that probably had nothing to do with her family's state of mourning. That mouth said: "What is it, *matri*?"

"Go get the photographs they took of your father for your grandparents' golden anniversary."

Her Italian was riddled with terms in dialect.

Then, with a glance in my direction, she added: "That's Rosalia, *la grande*: my elder daughter. We have the *nica* at home, too." The younger girl.

Rosalia came back with three color photographs in her hand. Her eyes were glistening. In the first picture that she held out to me, Giovanni Neglia was dressed in the same dark-brown suit he'd been wearing when he was murdered. The same tie. His wardrobe, I decided, was minimalist.

A good-looking man, without a doubt. A face that he'd left as an inheritance for his daughter, *"la grande."* The elder. Perfect proportions, bright eyes.

Rosalia gave her mother the second and third photographs as well. Just like the first, but here Neglia was lifting a glass under the affectionate eyes of his buxom spouse.

"Your husband…"

"He was good as gold."

"Sure he was. But he was a thief."

"Yes, but he was an honest thief."

I looked at her closely. This woman was the embodiment of the Sicilian spirit.

"What do you mean by that?"

"That he was careful not to hurt people."

But he must have hurt someone—he must have done some kind of *danno*, broken some fundamental rule, I mused, if they'd decided to separate his head from his body. I kept the thought to myself.

"Signora Cosima, you are certainly right. But in the recent past, by any chance…"

"Nothing. Nothing's happened 'in the recent past,' as *vossia* likes to say."

Rosalia was standing, listening. She went back into the other room, where her sister awaited her.

"Could you please tell me who your husband's friends are—excuse me, were?"

"Giovannuzzo grew up in Porticello. His father was a fisherman, they had a *muzzareddu*, you know, a small motorboat. They went out for squid. Or else saltwater sunfish. He grew up down at the harbor with his brother, Castrenze, who's older than him."

"Where is Castrenze now?"

"Here in Palermo. He works at the Vucciria market, he's still working in seafood: he sells tuna roe."

"But where, exactly?"

"On Piazzetta Caracciolo. He has a stand."

He worked at the Vucciria market, and he was still working in seafood. The man who sold me tuna roe. A middle-aged man who had told me all the details about how to salt and press the roe. He made it himself, in a small warehouse behind the Vucciria: "Hundreds of kilos of salt, it takes, and you have to make sure you turn the *balate*," the big stones used as weights in the roe press. I was a regular customer of Castrenze Neglia, the brother of Giovanni, whom I'd started to think of as Giovanni Decollato—St. John Beheaded—and I was discovering that fact at his widow's apartment.

"I may know your brother-in-law."

The woman shrugged. I don't think she cared if I knew him.

"The real problem now is for my daughters. Concetta! Rosalia! Come here, darling girls."

The two sisters entered the room slowly. The little one took her big sister's hand; she had pigtails. The two girls' eyes were filled with tears. In Rosalia's gaze I glimpsed the ferocity of a big cat, wounded. The little one, Concetta, reminded me of a lost puppy. They walked over to their mother, who tried to hold them both close without standing up. Her fat belly made that hard to do.

For an instant, I locked eyes with the big cat.

"Rosalia, forgive me. I didn't mean to bother you," I said.

She glared at me angrily. She turned around and took her little sister away with her: the show was over.

I thanked Signora Cosima. I promised her I'd keep her informed of any new developments in the investigation.

As I was leaving, I asked her what had happened to the French door.

"Oh, nothing; a truck came through a year ago. The street is narrow, and it took the balcony with it. Now we have to be careful when we open it."

I went back out onto Via Perpignano: the Vespa was still there; no trucks had come through.

● ● ● ● ●

"No question that it turned out beautifully: it looks fake."

Filippo Lombardo held out his arm to get a better view of the eight-by-ten-inch print. He took in the photograph of the head on the car seat with a pleased expression. "It's really a beautiful shot," he said, driving home the point. The aesthetics of death have never been in short supply in Palermo.

"What I don't understand is why there isn't so much as a drop of blood," he added.

I was in his workroom. I'd told him about my conversation with the three women of the Neglia family. I hadn't been especially generous with details about Rosalia. I'd just described her as a "typical Sicilian girl, in her late teens."

"We should photograph all three of them together. Imagine the headline: 'The Grief of the Women of St. John Beheaded.'" He laughed all by himself.

"Filippo, what are you laughing at?"

"Nothing: Can't a guy *babbiare* anymore?"

"Of course, you can kid around all you want, but those two girls lost their father not two days ago."

"Soft-hearted, eh? You're tender, just like a tasty green vegetable…" He twisted his two fingers as if drilling into his cheek: "*Appetitoso.*"

"Filippo, maybe I should go."

"Okay, forget I said a thing," he said. "If you ask me, though, we need to work hard on this case. It's very unusual: no Kalashnikovs, no car bombs, no .38 Specials, no tommy guns…De-cap-i-ta-ted. *Capisci?*"

"Of course I understand."

"You should read up on what it means, here, to chop off heads. There was a time when they put a rock in people's mouths for ratting."

"I've read Sciascia, I remember."

When I left, he was cleaning his Nikon flash couplers. I went back to my desk and called down to the archives.

"Anna, sorry, listen, I need a favor: Could you find me something in the encyclopedia about the ritual significance of a beheading?"

Annamaria Florio said nothing for several long seconds.

"Chopping off heads, right?"

"What did I just say?"

"You know that in China, Chairman Mao has forbidden beheadings."

"They're a crime in Italy, too, and you don't even have to be a Communist. Right?"

The Marxist-Leninist militant laughed through clenched teeth: "Why, what a comedian you've become."

"And you, with an abundance of comic research, see what you can find me about decapitation in various cultures. It would be great if you could find out what it means to cut someone's head off for a romantic and pessimistic people like the Sicilians."

"A romantic and pessimistic people? What you Sicilians need is a few Red Guards, my friend. Then see how pessimistic you still manage to be."

"Anna, you know that you and I are fundamentally in agreement. There's nothing I like better than steamed rice, and I have a soft spot for girls with almond-shaped eyes."

Before hanging up she said something that sounded like "asshole."

An hour later, there was a stack of Xeroxes on my desk.

I began to read: "In the ancient world, beheading was a method of execution used by the Egyptians and the Romans. Under the Roman Empire, it was a capital punishment reserved only for those who possessed Roman citizenship, because it was considered to be a quick form of death that did not entail any infamy; for slaves and highwaymen, in contrast, death was imposed by crucifixion. Beheading was also used widely in the Middle Ages and in the modern era. Until the eighteenth century, beheading was considered an honorable method of execution in Europe, available only to noblemen, while the bourgeois and paupers were punished with crueler methods, such as being drawn and quartered. In China, in contrast, it was considered the most infamous form of capital punishment, because according to the tenets of traditional religion, bodies were supposed to remain intact. In 1949, when the Communist regime took power, beheading was outlawed."

Annamaria had a point: Chairman Mao didn't like beheadings. What about the Mafia bosses? What meaning did they attribute to the headman's ax? There wasn't a hint in the papers on my desk. I'd need to talk to a scholar of Sicilian traditions, though I already had a pretty strong hunch: cutting someone's head off wasn't a sign of respect.

I suddenly remembered a night two years ago, outside police headquarters. A top-level mob boss, Masino Spatuzza, the owner of a fleet of dark-blue speedboats he used to bring the raw material for heroin, morphine, into Sicily, had been arrested after ten years on the lam. We journalists were waiting for him to do the perp walk—the *passerella*—in chains: from the high-security holding cells to the armored bus that would take him to Rome to stand trial. The boss appeared, flanked by two officers of the mobile squad: he was short, overweight, and furious, with enormous shackles on his wrists. I shouted to Filippo Lombardo: "Get that shot!" His flashgun flared. The boss climbed onto the bus as it pulled out, spitting at the television cameras focused on him.

Two minutes later I was surrounded by three guys about my age. They all had nasty glares and their shirts open to the last button above the navel. One of them was wearing a counterfeit pair of Ray-Bans, unnecessary at night, and they made him look like a killer. They said nothing, just surrounded me as Filippo was photographing the departing bus; he never noticed them. The tallest of the three stepped a little closer; I could smell the cigarette smoke on his breath. He whispered just four words to me: *"Ti scippiamo 'a tiesta."* *We'll take your head off.* I looked at him as if he were an extraterrestrial, and stepped away from that triangle of bad breath and impending violence, with my heart racing furiously. Message received.

The next morning, I talked about it with the head of the mobile squad: he sent a patrol car to park outside my house for a month. It hadn't been a very good idea to get on the nerves of the mob boss Spatuzza's three sons.

Ti scippiamo 'a tiesta. Their language. The symbolic meaning of the act.

"Come over here," said the news editor.

"At your service."

"Stop pulling my leg. Instead, why don't you tell me where we are with the severed head?"

"Wife, daughters, nothing much. A good husband, an exemplary father. The usual bullshit."

"Take a look at his criminal record."

"Already did it."

"Then go find out what he really did: talk to people, find out what they know."

"Got it. I'm on my way to Porticello. And I have plenty of phone tokens."

• • • • •

I slip my hand into my inside jacket pocket. I grab my BlackBerry, my little portable multimedia office, contained in five and a half ounces of high technology. I want to check the name of the capital of Ecuador. I open the browser and search on Google. Wikipedia:

*it's Quito, population 1,397,698, elevation above sea level 9,350
feet. I decide to trust the source.*

*There was a time when the only thing I trusted was a public
phone booth. And the bronze-colored phone tokens that cost fifty
lire. I still have a hundred or so, in a red cardboard box in a closet
somewhere. I've had them with me since my years in Palermo: you
never know.*

*Being a reporter in the early eighties was a pure activity, with
nothing else around it. No technology, no other means of communication. Those were the years when private television broad-
casting began in Italy; I worked for the station owned by my
newspaper. We were a high-energy group of news reporters busy
telling the story of the other Palermo, the city that refused to bow
to the inevitable fate of death by the Mafia. But the massacre was
under way. We weren't able to prevent the bloodbath: to tell the
truth, knowing now the way it turned out, I think not even Black-
Berrys could have stopped it.*

• • • • •

On the marble counter of the Porticello market sat two
swordfish heads that looked like a pair of cactuses: empty
eyes, giant, bony swords pointing straight up at the sky above
the green awning that shaded the fish stall. Farther along, two
old men sitting on the pavement of the wharf, near the market. They were mending fishing nets, working with a large
spindle and heavy thread, holding the mesh taut between
their toes and their mouths.

I locked the steering column of my Vespa and walked over.

"Forgive me for bothering you. Would you happen to
know where the Neglias live?"

Their hands stopped working. They looked at me.

"Neglia who?"

"Giovannuzzo's father. I know they had a motorboat."

"Yes, but Neglia *'ntisu Apuzza* or Neglia *'ntisu Cafè*?"

I didn't know how to answer that question. I knew that in town the families had nicknames known as *'nciurie*, which were used to identify a family much more than the surname: Was the man without a head an *apuzza*, a little bee, or a *cafè*? And what was the origin of the two nicknames?

"I have no idea," I said.

They went back to knotting their nets, clearly convinced that they were dealing with a functional moron.

The swordfish vendor had overheard the conversation.

"Who is it you're looking for?" he asked, wiping his bloody hands on his apron.

"The relatives of Giovanni Neglia."

"What could be easier? *Apuzza* and *Cafè* both live in the same building, in a second-floor apartment and a first-floor apartment. Down there, at Santa Nicolicchia."

He pointed out a little spit of land that enclosed the gulf, behind the breakwater. A pink building stood out against the bright-blue backdrop of the sea. Water behind it, water in front of it, and a ramshackle tenement building nearby.

"No, it's not the pink building," he said. "That belongs to people from Palermo. The Neglias live in the building next door." As he talked, he stroked the head of the largest swordfish, as if it were still alive. A caress of sincere fondness.

I thanked him and climbed back on the Vespa. Five hundred yards downhill, a distance I covered in neutral, breathing in the salt air. It was a warm day, and the sunlight was kind to the poverty of the fishing village.

The street door of the tenement where the Neglias lived was wooden. The brine had transformed it, over the years, into an object as unique as the driftwood that the tide tosses up onto the beach: beautifully deformed, inimitable. I rapped on the door with my knuckles. No reply.

"*Buon giorno*, anybody home?" I shouted.

From the second-floor window an old woman with a black scarf on her head looked out.

"*Signora*, excuse me, I'm looking for the Neglia family."

"*Apuzza* or *Cafè*?"

"Both. Which family do you belong to?"

"We're *Apuzza* Neglias."

"But are you by any chance related to Giovanni and Castrenze, who went to live in Palermo?"

"Those are *Cafè* Neglias. The sons of my cousin Peppino, who must be inside. Keep knocking, keep knocking."

The window swung shut.

At least now I knew who I was looking for.

I knocked again, louder this time. I shouted once or twice: "Signor Peppino!" After a few minutes, the wooden door creaked open. A sleepy old man in a sleeveless undershirt looked out.

"Who's looking for me?"

I told him that I worked for a newspaper. I asked if I could come in.

He nodded his head. The apartment was below street level, two steps down in total darkness.

The old man touched the parchment-like skin of his face. I heard the scraping of his hand's dry skin running over his two-day growth of whiskers. "I was asleep. We went out last night for squid. I got to sleep at six. *Si assettassi*," he said, pointing to a chair. "Would you like a *cafè*?"

I looked up, and in the dim light I made out ten glass mason jars filled to the top with coffee. Next to them, an assortment of Moka Express pots: one cup, three cups, six cups, and twelve. I started to understand the reason for the *'nciuria*.

"*Grazie*, thanks very much. Gladly."

"*Vossia* sells newspapers in Palermo, and you came all the way out here why?"

"For your son Giovanni."

"God rest his soul." He crossed himself.

"May he rest in peace," I added, with a look of dismay.

"And what does *vossia* want to know from me?"

"What was Giovanni doing in Porticello?"

"When he left he was just fifteen years old. He was tired of going out on the fishing boat with me. So was his brother, Castrenze, another fine piece of work."

"And what did Giovanni want to do?"

"What he's always done: be dishonest. He used to rob the other *picciriddi* when he was ten years old. He was clever and fast. But the idea of working? He wouldn't hear of it. Fishing is a life for men, not for the dishonest."

"And he was dishonest."

"How dare you say such a thing?"

"But you just said it yourself."

"I'm his father. But you, who the fuck are *you* to say that my son, a good Christian, God rest his soul, was dishonest?"

I realized I was heading down a dead-end street. I quickly covered my tracks, trying to become invisible: "Please forgive me, I was rude and thoughtless."

Just then, the Moka Express started to gurgle. Peppino Neglia stood up, turned off the flame, picked up a demitasse spoon, and stirred the freshly made espresso.

"If you don't do that, the strong coffee stays at the bottom and the *leggio*, the light coffee, the last to come out, floats on top. No, *'u cafè* should always be stirred."

He shoveled two spoonfuls of sugar into each cup and handed me one. I was out of the tunnel.

"*Grazie*, Don Peppino."

He smiled faintly at me. He'd decided that I was basically a good *picciotto*. A little rough around the edges, but harmless.

"You want to know what Giovannuzzo was doing?"

"If it's possible."

"Nothing. He stole in Palermo and every once in a while he'd come to see me and bring me a little something."

"What did he steal?"

"Honest things."

I looked at him fondly: the man had loved his son with all the love a father is capable of. A thief of a son, who stole *honest things*, as if he were a Robin Hood of the Conca d'Oro surrounding Palermo, a paladin of justice who restored fairness and order to the distribution of earthly goods. He saw things just the way his daughter-in-law did. But someone else begged to differ.

I drank my coffee, we talked about the price of squid, I thanked him, and I headed for the local police station.

The officer on duty took me for what I was: a source of irritation in the quiet of the winter seaside. He told me that the file his office had on Giovanni Neglia was practically empty. He went and got it, and there was only one prior report, sent from police headquarters in Palermo, for a break-in that took place on Corso Calatafimi. Nothing much stolen; no evidence, only suspicions; nothing solid against Neglia. I thanked the man and left him to his contemplation of the winter calm.

I went home, convinced I'd only wasted my time and enjoyed a good cup of coffee. I'd had worse days than that.

• • • • •

"There's a *signorina* downstairs for you," Saro, the doorman, called up to tell me.

"Who is it?"

"She says her name is Rosalia."

"Send her up."

I had started the afternoon with a pile of papers on my desk: the notes of the past year, to be sifted through. What should be kept? What should be tossed out? Which of those notes would prove useful in the future? I had no idea. I was rummaging through that dusty mountain in search of some clue to its usefulness. I was tempted to keep it all: I was a rookie reporter.

As I was reading back through the notes on my pointless journey to Porticello, the young quasi–Claudia Cardinale materialized in front of me. She was wearing a gray coat over a black knit dress. He eyes were made up to go with her mouth. Her mouth, the only dot of color on her oval face, was the natural pink that I remembered.

"I'm Rosalia Neglia, do you remember me?"

She had a gray purse clutched in one hand; it seemed to vanish into her overcoat.

I got to my feet.

Of course I remembered her. Her eyes, filled with rage and tears. Her hand, in which her little sister's hand had found a nest.

"We were on a first-name basis."

"You're right. It's just that I didn't know if you still remembered, whether I'd made an impression."

An indelible one. Like an embossed seal on a page in a book. But all I said was: "Yes, I remember you perfectly."

"My mother doesn't know that I'm here."

"Has something happened?"

Rosalia was standing in front of me, on the other side of the linoleum desktop heaped high with papers.

"I have some things to tell you, maybe someplace quiet." And, jutting out her chin, she indicated my three colleagues sitting at their desks on that sleepy afternoon. The newsroom had never been quieter.

"If you like, we can go upstairs to the room the photographers use. At this hour of the day there shouldn't be anyone there."

"Macari."

I translated the word in my mind: "Yes, *grazie.*"

I ushered her in. The reporter covering politics, Pippo Suraci, leapt to his feet as we went by, introducing himself with a certain unctuousness. As long as I'd known him, I'd never seen him miss a chance to take the hand of a young woman entering the newsroom: pretty or ugly, he shook hands with them all, blithely indifferent to his own sweaty palm. And Rosalia was the prettiest one ever to have set foot in our workplace. All she said was: "Pleasure to meet you." I placed a hand on her back and pushed lightly, to move her past Suraci. We climbed the stairs.

On the third floor, the photographers' room was, as I'd hoped, deserted. All the same, when I'd chosen that as a private place to have a conversation, I'd neglected to take into account the personality and habits of Filippo Lombardo. As soon as I opened the door, the severed head of Rosalia's father appeared before me, on the far wall. I quickly shut the door, asking her to be so kind as to wait for a moment.

"I just have to put something away."

She gave me a blank look, but didn't object.

I walked in, took the photograph off the wall, and hid it in the drawer with the unused AGFA developing paper. Then I let her in.

She put her overcoat on the table where Filippo laid out his prints when they were dry. Her dress, black for mourning, revealed her shape, reminding me of Angelica in *The Leopard*. I couldn't keep my eyes off the full curves of her bosom.

"What is it, Rosalia?"

"You have to help me. I need to know why they did what they did to my father."

"The police are investigating. I'm just a journalist."

"They'll never find out anything. They don't care enough. But I need to know."

"I understand: the pain a daughter would feel..."

"You don't understand. It's not just the pain. My mother says that this is an enormous disgrace. But I want to understand what was such a big disgrace. A person has to know why. It's the only way that I can ask forgiveness."

She picked up her purse. She opened it and pulled out a handkerchief: her eyes were dry, but she'd gotten it out just in case.

"Why do you have to ask forgiveness?"

"I don't know. But taking a father's head off takes the children's dignity with it."

I was starting to understand.

Then she added: "And I want it back, my dignity. I'm eighteen years old; one day, perhaps, who knows when, I want to get married myself. Who's going to marry the daughter of the guy whose head they cut off?"

I looked at her fondly. A girl dressed in mourning, nicely made up, had come to me in search of the dignity that a headsman's ax had robbed from her. I thought of the despair inhabiting a city where lives ripened like this, the pain of a daughter who couldn't simply mourn her murdered father, but was also forced to worry about the need for social redemption that such an atrocious death imposed upon her. I hated those mean streets, those cruel codes of behavior, that violence.

I walked over to her. I'd been silent, and the absence of words had defused the dramatic nature of the situation. Her mouth was quavering faintly. She might have felt like crying, but she didn't.

My fingers brushed hers.

"All right, Rosalia: I'll help you. Even if the police won't do anything, I'll give it a try."

It was she who took my hand. She squeezed it until it hurt; she bit her lower lip until it turned pinker still. Then she let me go. She put her overcoat back on and headed down the stairs.

"Come to my apartment in half an hour," she said as she was leaving. "My mother's gone out with my sister: there's something I want to show you."

At the front desk we ran into the news editor. He looked us up and down.

"Life is good, eh?"

The stupidity of that wisecrack crashed helplessly against the gaze of her black eyes. She wasn't a pretty girl paying a call: Rosalia was the victim of several millennia of Sicilian ideas. But then, how could he know that?

• • • • •

She refused to come with me on the Vespa.

"I'll see you there; I'll take the bus."

Of course, I got there before she did. I waited a few doors down the street, leaning against the wall. Via Perpignano was a main thoroughfare channeled, rushing, through a narrow alley, an artery choked by the city's massive cholesterol. The cars were inching forward in single file, bumper to bumper, from both directions. A Fiat 128 tried to get through ahead of an Alfa Romeo 1750 that was turning off Palermo's ring road, the Circonvallazione. The two cars faced off, radiator to radiator. The two drivers shot each other frosty glares: neither of them said a word. They sat there in silence, both gripping the steering wheel white-knuckled, as if fighting telepathically. Neither wanted to fight: each just wanted to win. I pondered the fact that in the streets of Palermo, no one started a fight, for the simple reason that if a fight were to break out, someone would inevitably be killed. And no one was really willing to commit murder over a traffic jam. Back then, there were so many other more respectable opportunities, such as heroin smuggling, the arms racket, robberies, the gang war for Mafia supremacy, crimes of passion, exemplary punishments. Cars were like dumb, useful mules, and nobody was willing to kill for a mule's sake.

From Piazza Principe di Camporeale I saw the silhouette of an oncoming bus, the same one Rosalia had boarded.

It stopped fifty feet away. She got out, tightening the belt around her gray overcoat, opened the door to her building, and, as she closed it behind her, shot me a glance. I was going to have to wait a few minutes before going upstairs. I saw the bus speed away, rocking wildly, narrowly missing a balcony.

The door clicked open.

I found her framed in the doorway, her eyes blacker than the darkness.

"Come here and I'll show you."

I followed her into her bedroom. Two beds, side by side. She sat down on the bed by the window; I heard the noise of cars going by on Via Perpignano.

"How can you sleep with this racket?"

"It's the noise of my whole life. We've always been here."

From a drawer in the nightstand that separated the two beds, she pulled out something small, wrapped in a rag.

"My father gave this to me a month ago."

She pulled open the rag and I saw a gold chain, marine link, heavy, glistening: it looked new.

"I cleaned it myself; it's my dowry."

The chain had an oval pendant, also gold. I turned it over: it was a reproduction of a woman's leg, in low relief.

An ex-voto.

"Rosalia, do you know what this is?"

"A leg, what else would it be? My father gave it to me because he used to say that I had the most beautiful legs on earth."

"Where did he get it?"

"One morning, he came home from work with two watches and this necklace. He never told us where he'd been. He always said the same thing: just don't worry, I've been careful. One time he brought Mamma a blender with a big glass jar. It needed cleaning. The night before, someone had made fava bean soup in it, and once the beans are dry they're almost impossible to get off."

I examined the pendant more closely. I'd seen something similar once at the sanctuary on Monte Pellegrino. Actually, hundreds of similar things. Lots of people left phrases of gratitude next to their ex-votos—for grace received—so that anyone who wanted to know could read about the family's devotion to the Santuzza.

Saint Rosalia.

"This is a copy of an ex-voto."

She twisted her full lips in a quizzical grimace: "What's that supposed to mean?"

"That the night he gave you this necklace, he took it from someone who may have left an ex-voto to Saint Rosalia. An ex-voto for a grace received. Someone who might have also written their name on it. That's the only hope we have of finding the rightful owner of this necklace; this is our one chance of understanding why what happened happened."

The girl nodded. She wrapped the necklace in the rag, put it in her gray purse, and said to me: "Let's go there now."

It was almost dark.

"No, Rosalia. At this hour, the sanctuary is already closed. I have to go home, and your mother and sister are probably on their way home, too. Let's do it tomorrow. I'll come pick you up in the morning on my Vespa at Piazza Principe di Camporeale: eight o'clock, at the bus stop."

She put down her purse. She said: "All right." Her eyes were midnight black, her pink lips illuminated that beautiful face of hers in the dim light.

She saw me to the door. We didn't touch; our two *ciaos* hung in the air.

•••••

When I got home, the apartment was cold. The aromas that came from the kitchen seemed like a spicy breeze wafting toward me. Oregano.

"*Ciao, amore mio,*" Lilli whispered, placing her lips on mine. "I'm making a breaded roast, the *arrosto panato.*"

She was wearing an apron with a tuxedo print that made her look both funny and sexy at the same time.

"Where's everyone else?"

"They went to get a glass of wine from Di Martino. They'll be back soon. I told them I was making a roast."

She went back into the kitchen. I tagged along behind her, embracing her from behind, hugging her tight.

"You know there's meat in the pan," she warned me.

"Turn the flame down low, you can turn it off if you want. I need you now."

She turned off the stove and turned around. Our fingers knit together down low, our hands on her hips, our mouths came together completely breaded, like tender, juicy roasts. A kiss that tasted of oregano and sweetness. A kiss long enough to study the way we were, to tell each other about our days. A kiss that we'd all like to give and receive, every day, when the lights go down low.

Lilli rested her head in the hollow of my shoulder. I smelled the perfume of her hair. I kissed her gently, the way you might kiss a newborn baby.

"*Amore mio,*" I whispered to her.

She smiled at me and pulled away.

"I have to finish the roast: the others will be back soon."

She turned the flame back on under the skillet, to low, and resumed cooking the four veal chops that she'd dipped in oil and then in a breading flavored with salt, pepper, and oregano. It had to cook excruciatingly slowly, to keep from burning the breadcrumbs.

I changed into a blue crewneck sweater. I looked for some wine and found only a bottle of "black" Pachino without a label. I'd bought it with Fabrizio at a winery near Ragusa, on a road trip the previous summer.

"Lilli, you want a glass?"

I heard her say yes just as Serena and Fabrizio came in.

"*Ciao*, journalist," Serena said, shaking out her dark hair, which had been flattened by the motorcycle helmet. The two of them were the only people in Palermo who wore helmets. "Fabri, look what's happened to my hair," she pretended to cry.

He tousled her ridiculously flat hair, which looked as if it had been licked by a large cow.

"You're beautiful all the same."

It was the truth.

"Lilli told us that she was making *arrosto panato*, and she kept her promise," said Fabrizio, sniffing the air in an exaggerated fashion.

It was a simple evening. I just wanted to avoid thinking about Rosalia's fears. Serena pulled out Scrabble; I put a Paolo Conte record on: we tried playing with nothing but words from his lyrics. Fabrizio won with a stunning laydown of "*barbarica*." Nine letters. So long that it wasn't even covered by the rules.

Cicova was on the sofa, in a drifting dream state, purring. I thought of a phrase that a classmate of mine in high school, a young woman, had copied into my desk diary. She told me that this was something I should learn by heart: "I want in my own home: a wife of sound reason, a cat among the books, friends in every season, without whom I cannot live." It was a French poem. That night I understood its meaning.

Later, in bed, Lilli told me about a comic book that she was carrying in her toy store. A monstrous and invincible super-hero called Goldrake—known in English as Grendizer. He rocketed through space, fired rays from his body, and wore a mask that struck fear into villains throughout the universe. She told me that the kids only wanted his books, his action figures. She had to stock Goldrake in her shop, but she found those products repellent.

I tried to comfort her: "The whole world is changing. Don't you go changing, too, please." She kissed me lightly. I wrapped my arms around her; her feet were cold. She turned around and we spooned together, her legs pulled up so the bottoms of her feet pressed against my thighs: I quickly warmed her up. She fell asleep with my hands wrapped around her chest like a bra.

I couldn't get to sleep. I kept seeing Rosalia's face at the paper that day, her stifled sobbing. She was asking me for jus-tice and that was something I couldn't give her. I felt Lilli's warmth beside me as she breathed quietly, fast asleep. The two women were opposite extremes. Two young women at the antipodes of life in Palermo, alternate faces of a city that was splitting me in two. One and the other. Dark Rosalia, fair Lilli. The complexity of a life based on honor, balanced against the simplicity of a quiet existence, simple sentiments, tenderness, and cold feet.

I lived in that chaotic equilibrium that comes from being around two women very different from each other. I could easily have loved them both, if I'd only had a second life to live. But then and there I knew I couldn't do it; I knew that my place was in that perfect fit that Lilli's body created with mine. Rosalia was the mirror in darkness, the reflection of another life, the need to be a man.

I fell asleep imagining myself in a fitting room at the shop of my father's tailor. I was looking at myself in the triple mirrors. In the central mirror I saw myself, in a navy-blue jacket; in the left-hand mirror I saw Lilli, nude; in the right-hand mirror, Rosalia, dressed in mourning.

• • • • •

The sky was streaked with dark clouds; this promised to be a tough morning. The cold winter air weighed down upon the city, as if it had been unloaded by a gantry crane from a container ship. I shivered during the short Vespa ride from my house to the newspaper. It was seven in the morning. I knew that right then Lilli and Cicova were both stretching and yawning; soon they would both fall asleep again.

Saro welcomed me with his usual greeting: "Sleepy eyes, sleepy eyes." I said nothing. "Chilly eyes, or eyes of love," I would have liked to say to him. I just smiled: I was shivering with cold and in a wintry mood.

I went to my desk and saw my boss lighting an MS cigarette. I tried to guess how many espressos he'd already thrown back, how many cigarettes he'd already sucked down.

I waved my hand deferentially in his direction: in the morning at the paper, chitchat really was cut to the bone.

He let me take off my dark-blue jacket, get comfortable, open the morning paper—the large-format daily that had five times our circulation. Then he said: "Come here, let's talk about that head."

"Today I ought to find out something more. I'm going up to Monte Pellegrino."

"*Bravo*, maybe the Santuzza will grant you a grace and provide you with a scoop."

"There's something important I need to check out…"

"Something important you can't tell me."

"That's right. Let's just say I'm superstitious. But I promise, the minute I know something for sure, I'll look for a phone…"

I ran to my desk, grabbed cigarettes, ballpoint pen, lighter, and notepad, shoved everything into the pockets of my jacket, and headed straight for Piazza Principe di Camporeale. I had time for a cup of coffee and a cigarette under the portico. Fifteen minutes of peace.

At 8:00 a.m. I parked my Vespa thirty feet from the bus stop and settled down to wait for Rosalia. She came toward me, wrapped in her gray overcoat, her hair pulled back, wearing a pair of dark pants and low-heeled shoes. Her face was free of makeup, and she looked around her, hard-eyed, though her gaze softened when she spotted me.

"*Ciao*, Rosalia."

She responded to my greeting, and then looked around.

"We'll go on my Vespa, is that all right?"

"Yes," she replied. She touched her hips, as if to adjust her overcoat, which didn't need any adjusting.

"Have you ever ridden on a Vespa?"

"Of course."

I started the motor; she climbed on behind me and wrapped her arms around my chest while we were still standing still. I felt her body pressed against my back; I sensed the shapes that I'd imagined in that knit dress of hers.

"I won't go too fast, I promise."

"*Grazie.*"

She loosened her grip, and I was almost sorry she did.

Twenty minutes later, we were climbing the slopes of Monte Pellegrino. The road to the sanctuary turned off the Via della Favorita, the main thoroughfare that led to Mondello. The road was popular with young couples in search of seclusion as well as speed demons putting their customized Fiat 500 Abarths through uphill time trials, a sequence of hairpin turns and tunnels that went all the way to the summit of the mountain overlooking Palermo. Parked cars lined the tunnels, their windows lined with newspapers: there was lovemaking going on behind the newsprint, on reclinable car seats, with the thrill of the forbidden.

High atop Monte Pellegrino stood the Castello Utveggio, a castle made of red stone. Just beneath was the grotto where Rosalia Sinibaldi met her death in 1165: she was a Norman noblewoman, a descendant of Charlemagne who refused to be taken as the wife of a local count. She chose instead to cut her hair, run away, and live as a hermit in that grotto, where she died a virgin. The rocky cavern where her corpse was found by a group of intrepid pilgrims was eventually transformed, over the centuries, into a place of worship, the site of a saint cult that verged on paganism. We were heading for the Grotto of Santa Rosalia, fondly known as La Santuzza, the beloved patron saint of Palermo, where she was celebrated every year in a *festino* that lasted almost a week, as she had been for the past eight hundred years.

It was 8:30 when we pulled up to the sanctuary. We were alone there except for a small knot of Germans, the only people on earth who take the job of tourism seriously, eschewing the frivolous pleasures other nations seem to find in it. As the guide lectured them, we ventured inside as if to pray to the saintly relics.

The walls of the grotto glittered with silver and gold: thousands of ex-votos had been hung up for grace received, transforming the grotto into a metallic cavern, exquisite and glittering. The caretakers of the sanctuary, displaying a love for tidiness and order, had arranged the ex-votos according to categories: at the top right were those depicting brains and heads; on the left were internal organs: heart, liver, kidneys, stomach, and gall bladder; last of all, arms and legs. Hundreds of limbs depicted in ovals and rectangles of precious metals. Many of them featured an engraving on the nameplate: "The Di Liberto family placed this, in gratitude, for grace received"; "The Spampinato family made this, for grace received"... Each ex-voto had its own style of engraving.

Rosalia pulled the necklace wrapped in a rag out of her purse. We examined it carefully, looking for similarities with any of the ex-votos in the area dedicated to legs.

"Let's focus on the bigger ones," I said. "If the copy was attached to a gold necklace, the family that had it made was probably well-to-do, so they might well have chosen an expensive ex-voto."

The biggest plaques of gold and silver were on our left, low down. The Germans kept asking their guide questions.

One of them pointed his finger at a boat in a storm engraved on a silver plaque: there were even ex-votos expressing gratitude for surviving a shipwreck.

Rosalia was making comparisons, while I tagged along behind her.

The oval medallion dangling from the stolen necklace had a border of interwoven laurel branches. At its center was a leg that could have belonged to a Hollywood diva. The engraver who'd done it clearly had an artistic touch: a fifties realist, from the school of Renato Guttuso. A shapely thigh, a slender calf, a graceful foot. All that was missing was the signature of the Maestro of Bagheria: Guttuso.

Rosalia pointed to an ex-voto down low, almost touching the floor.

"Look at this one, there's a close resemblance."

I knelt down beside her. Our shoulders touched. I held her hand, which held the pendant, and I laid it over the ex-voto hanging from the rock. One was an enlargement of the other.

We'd found it. I read out loud: "The Pecoraino family placed this ex-voto in gratitude for the grace received by Filomena—May 8, 1981." I scribbled on my notepad: "Pecoraino," "Filomena," and the date. Three illegible scrawls. Rosalia looked down at the sheet of paper and asked: "What on earth did you just write?"

"Nothing, just notes for myself."

She grabbed my arm with a dazzling gleam in her dark eyes. Being close to the other Rosalia, her namesake, had given her a concentration of distilled energy that, as we zoomed along the hairpin curves leading back to the Via della Favorita, was unleashed upon my chest, both hands holding tight as if they were a gentle vise. Every time the Vespa braked, I could feel her bosom press against my back. I silently thanked the Santuzza.

· · · · ·

At noon I was sitting across from Antonio Gualtieri, after dropping Rosalia off at the bus stop for Piazza Principe di Camporeale.

On his desk was a copy of *Tuttosport*, with a headline about Michel Platini on the front page.

"Antonio, he can do it, he can do it."

"Keep it up and I'll have you arrested."

Platini was Juventus's star player, and he was in line for the player of the year award.

"I know that you're not allowed to joke about the Pallone d'Oro, but I'm saying it in all sincerity."

"It might be safer for you if we stick to murders: What do you want to know?"

"Who are the Pecorainos?"

"Pecoraino who?"

"I can't tell you that. A daughter or a wife ought to be named Filomena. This may have something to do with the severed head. I saw a necklace with a pendant. Do you think you could do me a favor—"

I didn't get a chance to finish.

"Zoller!" he shouted, as if the office were going up in flames.

The inspector came rushing in.

"At your orders!"

"This young friend of mind wants to be an investigator. You wouldn't happen to have a spot for him on your squad, would you?"

"*Dottore,* if you say so…" Zoller replied with a tone of resignation.

"You see, not even Zoller wants you. Do you really have to keep digging into the story of that head?"

I said nothing about Rosalia and the promise I'd made her.

"I'm obsessed with it. My boss says that it's such a weird murder it boosts circulation."

The pity ploy seemed to work.

"All right. Zoller, let's see if we can help this young man who wants to be famous. Check into this Federica…"

"Filomena Pecoraino."

"Filomena. But what does this woman have to do with the murder?"

"I really have no idea. Maybe nothing. But if I want to figure it out, it's important to find out who she is."

Gualtieri looked me up and down. "Here's the young gumshoe again," he said.

Zoller left the office with a brisk "I'm on it, sir!" in the direction of his commanding officer.

The policeman standing watch outside came in with two espressos. We talked about the Palermo team and how it was making me suffer, and about Juventus and how it was kindling dreams of championships. In those ten minutes, the phone must have rung a dozen times. I heard him say: "No, *you* go to hell, asshole!" then, "No, it's not his shift," then, "All right, he's authorized to use his Ciao moped to follow the guy," then, "The Greco clan? Well, what do you want me to do about it?" and finally, "No, I don't think I'll be home tonight earlier than ten. Calamari will be fine." Fragments of conversations with subordinate officers, judges, the chief of police, noncommissioned officers, and his wife. Gualtieri's telephone was a nightmare with a ring tone.

Zoller came back.

"*Dottore*, I think I've found it. Pecoraino, Filomena, born in Palermo on August 10, 1970, died in Palermo on February 16, 1982. The daughter of Pecoraino, Ruggero, born in 1947, the brother-in-law of Incorvaia, Salvatore, born in 1944, fugitive from the law, the capo of the *mandamento* of Partanna Mondello according to the testimony of the informant Gaspare Fascetta."

Giovanni Neglia had stolen the wrong thing from the wrong apartment. I told Gualtieri about the stolen pendant with the copy of the ex-voto; I told him what I'd seen in the grotto atop Monte Pellegrino, without mentioning the fact that I'd been there with Rosalia.

He thanked me. By that time, he'd come up with an idea of what had happened.

I went back to the newspaper in a hurry, just in time to write a front-page piece. The headline read: "Mystery of the Severed Head: There's a Lead."

I made no mention in the article of either family, Pecoraino or Incorvaia. I simply mentioned a copy of an ex-voto that had provided the investigation with a lead. I quoted Rosalia Neglia, the bereaved daughter, as saying that she needed to find out the truth. "You can't live with the burden of doubt," she said, in conclusion. As if she were a Kantian philosopher. Words she'd never said, but that I had thought. As in so many cases of shoddy journalism, I'd attributed my own thoughts to the person I was interviewing, in place of her own. *Nice work*, I said to myself as I reread what I'd written.

I spent the afternoon at the paper, looking over my notes from the piazza in front of the train station, Porticello, the mobile squad, and Monte Pellegrino. I couldn't figure out the reason for the ex-voto: the little girl had died in the end. No grace had been received. As is so often the case, neither the doctors nor the Santuzza had done a bit of good. Then why had the Pecoraino family paid to engrave not one but two gold ex-votos?

I asked Annamaria, my friend the archivist, to find me the death notices for February 17, 1982. The day after little Filomena died. An hour later, there was a Xerox on my desk.

Papà Ruggero and Mamma Maria, in an agony of grief,

mourn the loss of

FILOMENA PECORAINO

age 12, taken from this life, an innocent child, after terrible suffering.

May God embrace her in glory.

Our gratitude goes out to the physicians of the Children's Hospital,

especially Dr. Rosa Buttitta.

There was a lead. Just like it said on our front page.

• • • • •

The Children's Hospital looked like a Chilean penitentiary. Gray, cube-shaped, all it lacked were machine-gun nests at the corners and barbed wire all around it.

You could feel the despair of the place on your skin, as if it were a uniform. A mother hit me with the wheelchair she was pushing: the little girl sitting in it looked at me glassy-eyed, her face deformed by a spasm. At the front desk, I asked for Dr. Rosa Buttitta.

"Do you have an appointment with the head physician?" a fat man with white hair and a copy of *La Settimana Enigmistica* draped over the telephone asked me.

"No, I wanted to see Dr. Buttitta."

"Which means you want to see the head physician."

"Oh, I see. Sorry."

I'd gotten off on the wrong foot. I introduced myself and the receptionist shoved *La Settimana Enigmistica* aside, making a call to the ward upstairs and reporting that a journalist was asking to come up.

"It's a sad case, about a little girl who died," I suggested.

The receptionist covered the receiver with one hand and froze me to the spot by whispering: "Believe me, all our cases are sad."

On the other end of the line, someone said something.

"All right, I'll send him up."

He hung up the phone. He would have been much happier calling security and having me tossed out on the street.

The ward was on the third floor. The sign at the entrance, plastic, said: GENERAL MEDICINE 1—CHIEF PHYSICIAN DR. ROSA BUTTITTA. With an X-Acto knife, someone had carved into the plastic: "Ring Bell."

I obeyed instructions and rang, even if there was no need: the door was open.

There was a hustle and bustle of nurses. At the end of the corridor I noticed a tall woman in a lab coat, with fluffy blonde hair, flanked by two young men, likewise dressed in white. I stopped a male nurse pushing a gurney.

"Is that the head physician?" I asked, pointing at the woman.

He nodded his head and moved away.

I walked toward her. She had just dismissed her two assistants and was walking back into her office.

I introduced myself.

"Ah, the journalist. Come with me."

We walked into her office. A simple room with a white metal desk, a sofa in burgundy Naugahyde, and a glass-front cabinet for the medicines that pharmaceutical reps gave her. The wall behind the desk was adorned with a large baroque oil painting, a landscape with red highlights. A second canvas was hanging next to a Swedish bookcase: it depicted a man from behind, looking out over the sea from the rocks. An image that could contain, depending on the eyes of the beholder, either hope or despair.

"Do you like art?"

"It helps me to survive," she replied, with a faint but courteous smile.

"I could never do the work you do."

"I chose it at age twenty. Now I'm fifty-six. With these hands, I've touched pain and suffering of every kind."

She held her hands out to me: her fingernails were painted with Mavala, a product to stop nail biting.

"Doctor, forgive me. I need to ask what you remember about a little girl who, sadly, is no longer with us."

I blushed at the hypocrisy of the euphemism. This wasn't a woman who needed false sanctimony.

"Tell me the name and the date of death."

"Filomena Pecoraino, February 16, 1982."

She called an assistant and told him to bring her the clinical file.

"She was my patient. I remember. She had a bone tumor that began in her right leg. She passed away in the orthopedic ward. But I followed her case throughout her illness. They diagnosed the tumor when she was ten. A year of chemo, and she seemed much improved. Her parents thought she was cured."

And they offered their thanks to St. Rosalia, I added in my mind.

It was all becoming clearer.

"Do you remember ever seeing Filomena wearing a gold necklace?"

"She never wanted to take it off. Every time I came to see her, I'd joke about her jewelry. Her parents had given it to her. They'd told her it ensured that Saint Rosalia, the Santuzza, would protect her. I've never encouraged that sort of thing among my patients. Still, of course, fairy tales for children…"

She broke off. Her eyes focused on a point midway between the glass-front pharmaceuticals cabinet and the bookshelf. The dirty white of the wall.

"Did they call you when she died?"

"Yes, they wanted me to be with them. The little girl was half-unconscious, because of all the drugs she was on; she died in the evening, holding her *mamma*'s hand. I remember that at first the *signora* couldn't seem to cry. She silently took the necklace off Filomena's neck. She put it in her purse, walked away from the bed like a robot. Then she fainted."

• • • • •

Every one of us keeps relics, and our memories in particular brim over with them: fragments of conversations, images, states of mind, little objects. We venerate them as if they were a saint's thighbone. Our own personal saints: secular, misbelieving, carnal saints. I once knew a girl who carried a rock with her everywhere she went. She kept it in her stylish leather Tolfa handbag. It was a small, smooth stone, from a distant beach. A hippie who was in love with her had picked it up on a Pacific beach. She was never without her South Sea stone: "It tells me where to go, it keeps me in equilibrium." Those were years of starry sentiments, words plucked out of the skies above, crystal-clear eyes.

Filomena's necklace only remained in Maria Pecoraino's purse for the time it took to get home from the Children's Hospital. She wrapped it in an embroidered handkerchief, and once she was back in her bedroom, she decided where to keep it: she opened the Empire-style drop-front dresser that stood at the foot of her bed, pulled out a small red velvet box from inside the drop front, and slipped the necklace into it. She snapped the box shut: that sound was a foreshadowing of the closing of the small white casket. Then she hid the key in the top drawer, under her handkerchiefs.

It was February 16, 1982. Almost two years later, the Empire-style dresser would be rifled through by the nimble gloved fingers of a thief who only stole *honest things*.

• • • • •

I returned home with a picture in my mind: a view over the shoulder of the man looking out to sea. Hope or despair? I wavered between the two, thinking back over the whole story as it slowly reassembled itself. What hope had Giovanni Neglia had of surviving his own fatal misstep? And what kind of despair lay in wait for Rosalia? The despair of truth? Should I have told her the whole truth? Left out the details? Explained to her that a little girl had died young and a mother would never again be a whole person? Would she have understood? Would it have been enough for Rosalia to understand the horrible cruelty suffered by her father and her family?

I sensed the intolerable disproportion between the offense and the punishment, a punishment inflicted in the name of a code of justice that was as pitiless as it was primitive. I needed to think it over, choose carefully the words to use with her, and in my paper.

I needed Lilli; I needed her gentle sweetness: I needed to get my thoughts back into proportion.

"*Mio amore*, where have you been?"

She welcomed me at the door with a warm hug. I felt that warmth loosen the hardest knots inside me: I would have liked to curl up and go to sleep inside her.

"The story of the severed head."

"You always see such horrible things."

"I'm a beat reporter: I have no choice."

"Do you want something to drink? Fabrizio bought some beer."

I heard "Father and Son" wafting in from the living room. Lilli loved Cat Stevens; Serena hated him.

"*Grazie*, my sweet love."

She got out a quart bottle of Messina beer and a couple of glasses. We sat down on the brown sofa.

It's not time to make a change,
Just relax, take it easy.
You're still young, that's your fault,
There's so much you have to know.

I felt like crying. Lilli took my hand: she caressed it as if it were velvet, with the grain. I felt the warmth of her embrace spread through me again. That girl was my sunshine.

We drank our beer. Luckily, the next track came on: it was "Tea for the Tillerman." And Fabrizio and Serena came home.

"Journalist, you really are one lucky man."

I looked at her with a faint smile. Lilli said: "*Ciao*, Sere."

"Hey all!" said Fabrizio, displaying an enormous cardboard tray wrapped in pale-pink bakery paper.

"*Sfincione*," he said. A deep-dish Sicilian pizza, a specialty of Palermo. "We're celebrating tonight," he added.

"Celebrating what, Fabri?"

"Top scores on my business management test. A-plus-plus. You understand? Plus-*plus*!"

It had been a big hump to get over, as he'd explained to me at length. I was happy for him, and for us, because now we had a couple of kilos of warm aromatic *sfincione*.

The evening had found a new point of equilibrium. I took off Cat Stevens, and I put on "Young Americans." A little funky Bowie was an open window with a view of the future I was dreaming of, far away from the ferocity of Palermo.

• • • • •

The Mafia has always believed that control of a specific terri-tory is one of the foundations of real power. You're powerful only if you're in control, and only if everyone knows you're in control. In the spring of 1982, when Carabinieri General Carlo Alberto Dalla Chiesa was appointed the prefect of Palermo, a debate arose immediately over the powers that had been conferred on the leg-endary terrorist hunter, along with his new position. The debate didn't last long: the Italian state hadn't given Dalla Chiesa any real power. Everyone agreed on that point, even Dalla Chiesa himself, and he demanded an explanation from the man who had sent him down to Sicily, Interior Minister Virginio Rognoni. In return he received promises that were never kept, and no real power. Five months later, the Mafia assassinated the general, his wife, Emanuela Setti Carraro, and their driver, Domenico Russo. A resident of the quarter hung a pen-and-paper sign on the place where they were murdered: "Here died the hope of all honest Palermitans." It was temporarily true. But the murder of Dalla Chiesa also contained another truth, so well understood by the Mafia: you can't win if you don't have control. Dalla Chiesa was intelligent but helpless. Unlike the mob bosses who ordered his death.

The capi of Cosa Nostra not only had the power of control, but also had the duty to show they possessed it. Their murders had to make a point. Everyone had to understand. The Corleonese took the great leap forward: they brought the strategy of massacres to Palermo with a succession of car bombs and dynamite buried under the asphalt, and assaults on the highway; they introduced a degree of ferocity that had never been seen before. Cutting off a head was an obligatory phase in that escalation, in that delirium of murderous power. If life were a lecture, then the decapitation of Giovanni Neglia would represent the phrase "for example."

• • • • •

Castrenze Neglia finished covering the last vat of tuna roe with salt. His assistant helped him to put back the *balatone*, the large, smooth stone that weighed down the salt and roe in the press. He wiped the sweat off his face and scratched his head.

He thought about his brother, Giovannuzzo, his mouth pursed in a whisper on the front page of the newspaper: he felt like throwing up. He'd handed him over to his murderers; he'd betrayed him without thinking twice, bending his knee when Salvatore "Salvo" Incorvaia had made his demand, in the face of his brutal and ferocious extortion: "Castrenze, my darling boy, we know that he was the one who stole the necklace, the fences in the Borgo told us so. Bring him to us, and we'll beat him black and blue. You can go back to *travagghiare* with your tuna roe. And he'll have paid his debt to my cousins, the Pecoraino family. It's better for you to do it this way, believe me."

My darling boy. Those three words came out flat from between the thin grayish lips of Salvo Incorvaia. Castrenze was afraid of that man—so young, so evil. He answered yes with his eyes as he looked down. The next night he used some excuse to persuade Giovanni to come down to the fish market, behind the Cala. And there Giovanni found Salvo waiting for him, with an armed escort: two *picciotti*. Giovanni looked at his elder brother in bewilderment: he couldn't understand. Castrenze took two steps back, arched his eyebrows as if to say, "What can you do about it?" Castrenze knew that Giovanni was about to take a beating, that he was about to pay his debt in the coin of physical pain: but in Palermo, it's better never to leave a debt unpaid.

What can you do about it, Giovannuzzo?

He went home, certain he'd have to explain the next day that he'd done it for Giovanni's own good. A beating, a pounding, a clubbing, and then you're done. Anything, everything, but not a severed head on the front page of the newspaper, whispering over and over again: *You betrayed me, and you're my brother.*

His assistant left for the day. They'd replenished the salt on all the tuna roe. He washed his hands, picked up a pad of graph paper, and wrote a couple of lines in off-kilter block print, in a hybrid language all his own: IT WAS BEEN THE INCORVAIAS, DOWN AT THE SEEFOODE MARCKET. He folded the sheet of paper, slipped it into a yellow envelope, the kind you use to send certified letters, and wrote the address of the newspaper and the name of the reporter who'd written the articles about Giovannuzzo's murder, stamped it, and mailed it.

People in Palermo pay their debts.

• • • • •

A certified letter from an illiterate. There it sat, on my desk, tossed there by Saro as he was distributing the morning mail: in the name, address, and city, I counted five misspellings. I opened it. And my theory was confirmed: illiterates know everything.

I reread those two lines in block print. The Incorvaias: exactly. The Pecorainos' cousins. It was them, down at the seafood market.

I checked in with the news editor; we decided to turn the anonymous letter over to Gualtieri. I was looking for his direct number when the phone on my desk rang. The switchboard informed me that there was a girl who wanted to talk to me.

"Who is it?"

"She wouldn't say."

"All right, put her through."

I'd guessed who it was.

"*Ciao*, Rosalia."

She said nothing. I could hear her breathing.

"I have to talk to you. Could you come to Da Cofea, right away?" There was a mournful tone to her voice.

"I'm on my way."

I put the anonymous letter in my pocket, grabbed my cloth jacket, and galloped downstairs.

Eight minutes later I was pulling up outside the shop that sold the finest *brioche con gelato di caffè* ever produced in Palermo. Pastries filled with coffee-flavored gelato.

Rosalia was in the back, sitting at a little table. She wore seventies-style sunglasses with oversized lenses, in black plastic frames, and her gray overcoat; an appearance that overall seemed hardened, if that was possible. I sat down with her, and we ordered mineral water.

"You have to stop writing." Just like that, without preliminaries.

"*Ciao*, Rosalia. What's this all about?"

"You have to stop, you have to stop." Her voice broke, and she was sobbing.

"What's happened?"

She lifted her sunglasses, and she had a black eye, her left eye—bruised and swollen shut.

"A man, last night. He was waiting for me by the bus stop. He told me that if I wanted to know the truth, he'd be glad to tell me all about it. The way they'd told my father. I tried to run away, and he gave me a tremendous punch. I flew to the pavement. And he strolled away, in no hurry, lighting a cigarette."

I took her hand in mine. It was icy cold. She put her sunglasses back on, squeezed my fingers, and I saw a tear make its way past the barrier of the sunglass frames and streak its way down her cheek.

"I promised to help you, to find the truth so you could get your life back," I told her.

"I know you did. But now I'm afraid."

My mind went to the anonymous note in my pocket. The truth was written on it, and maybe I'd just have to keep it to myself. Maybe.

I moved my chair over closer to hers.

"Rosalia, you need to go away. You're a smart, beautiful, proud girl. Go on, get out of here, run away."

"I'm a daughter: I'm not going anywhere."

She let go of my hand. She stood up, adjusting her overcoat.

"But do me this favor: stop writing about what happened to my father."

I said yes, with the immediate rush of guilt that comes when you're a bad liar: I'd stop writing, but the police wouldn't stop investigating.

We said goodbye with a single kiss on the cheek, the way we do in Palermo. Then I watched her go. She didn't turn around. She'd given up.

• • • • •

In the late afternoon I went to see Gualtieri. I gave him the anonymous letter and told him about the threats and the violence targeting Rosalia. I asked him to take it easy. To keep it all under wraps. He asked me why.

"That girl would like to have a future," I tried to explain.

He eyed me curiously.

"If you ask me, the only future she can hope for is one where we catch the people who murdered her father and say just how things went. What do you say to that, young investigator?"

"Yes and no."

"Meaning what?"

"Antonio, you ought to know: in Palermo there's never a full yes, nor is there ever a direct no. The way we say things is *a trasi e nesci*, in and out, enter and exit. Forward and back, start and stop: never clearly in one direction."

"So what are we supposed to do, arrest a little bit and a little bit not arrest?"

"No, I'm just asking you to be discreet. Don't let the press write the whole truth about the beheading of her father."

"I don't know the whole truth yet."

"You'll find it, trust me. You start the way I did from the ex-voto to Saint Rosalia and this anonymous note. I could have thrown it away, but I brought it to you precisely because I want the truth to be told, but discreetly."

He was a Turinese cop in Palermo; but then and there he felt like a human being, the only human being, on Mars.

"Fine. I'll protect the girl."

I smiled gratefully. We chatted for a few more minutes about the soccer player Zbigniew Boniek and the coverage he got in *France Football*, and then I left.

The night sky was dark; there was a storm on its way. In the street, I felt the first few drops hit my face. I chained the Vespa to a lamppost near the door to my building. I needed a sense of safety.

Lilli was in the kitchen; Serena and Fabrizio were in their bedroom. Cicova rubbed his back against my left calf. I heard the slow notes of "Us and Them" from the living room, the intertwining voices of Gilmour and Wright. I'd landed back on my own happy planet, I was breathing the air of my own generation, there was shared DNA in our cells.

"Welcome home, *mio amore*," Lilli said, as I walked toward her down the hall. I hugged her so tight it took her breath away.

"I love you," I whispered, letting her catch her breath. She, too, was a daughter; I, too, was a son. We all were, in a place where the meaning of the word "family" is love today, horror tomorrow.

The evening slipped away peacefully, over a bowl of spaghetti and a few LPs of progressive rock. I did my best to forget about Rosalia's tears. I suggested we play a game of Trivial Pursuit. Two hybrid teams: Fabrizio and Lilli against me and Serena. We were quickly beaten: they knew everything, they were intolerable.

Lilli yawned and Serena and Fabri said *buona notte*. We went to bed, too.

I couldn't get to sleep. It wasn't the adrenaline; I'd exhausted that with Rosalia and Gualtieri. It was a sense of inadequacy with respect to my working days: I did my job, I dealt with death, I talked to policemen, women, little kids. I searched, I found, and I wrote. But I understood nothing. I couldn't see a reason why. A reason why there was another world, so different from the one I know that surrounded me, outside that apartment, a world that was "plus fourteen" away from Palermo. All it took was a train, a night in a sleeping car, and I'd see in the rest of Europe how different the late twentieth century was.

Lilli had fallen asleep with her arms around me, a sweet ball of wool, a tiny island of meaning.

I didn't turn off the lamp on the nightstand. In my hands I was holding a copy of *The Stories of F. Scott Fitzgerald*. I kept rereading the same two lines without registering a word. I decided to get up and do what I ought to have done at the end of the afternoon: write my piece about the death of Giovanni Neglia.

I pulled my pistachio-green Olivetti Lettera 22 typewriter out of its case, took out a sheaf of millimeter graph paper, and went into the dining room to keep from awakening Lilli. I sat down at the dinner table.

> The mystery of the severed head has been solved: Giovanni Neglia, age 50, was beheaded because he stole a necklace from the home of Ruggero Pecoraino, cousin of a Mafia boss. The necklace had belonged to his daughter, little Filomena, who died of cancer at age 12. The murder was committed by Salvatore "Salvo" Incorvaia, a mob boss with ties to the Corleonese clan and Pecoraino's brother-in-law.

In the eighty lines that followed, I gave an account of the murder and its solution, explaining that the beheading had taken place in the Incorvaias' warehouse, a place normally used for the decapitation of tuna. The head had been severed with a meat cleaver and then left to bleed out, hung up near the fish until it was drained of blood. The killer had then placed the body in the trunk of the car and had left the Ford Escort in front of the station to make the whole thing that much more evident, a clear and unmistakable lesson. I ended the piece with a reference to the suffering of the Neglia family.

I read it over. I crumpled it up and threw it in the trash.

I stretched out on the sofa and picked up a book of poetry by Giorgio Caproni that Serena had left on the coffee table. A postcard of the catacombs of the Capuchin monks book-marked page 81.

I opened the book and read from the beginning:

Amore mio, nei vapori d'un bar
all'alba, amore mio che inverno
lungo e che brivido attenderti!

My love, amid the fumes of a bar
at dawn, my love, such a long
winter, I shiver as I wait for you!

It was all too much. Too many different gazes, impossible to meet at that point of the night: Rosalia's black eyes, once again dark in her unconditional surrender; Lilli's blue eyes, transparent with gentle sweetness; the eyes, closed forever, of that bodiless head; the ferocious eyes of a man who chops, beheads, and bleeds out a human being. And now the sigh of those lines of verse, the certainty of a different world, far away, in the eyes of a man in love, waiting in a café at sunrise.

I shut the book and set it down. Cicova slowly came over to me. He pushed his nose against my whiskers. He wanted me to go on reading. I paid no attention to him, but I should have: cats are always right.

Place Names

The heart of Palermo is split into four parts by the inter-section of two main thoroughfares: Corso Vittorio Emanu-ele, also known as the Càssaro (from the Arabic "*qasr*," "the fortress"), a road first built by the Phoenicians to connect the port to the necropolis; and Via Maqueda, built at the end of the sixteenth century at the behest of the Spanish viceroy at the time, Bernardino de Cárdenas, Duque de Maqueda. The crossroads where the two main thoroughfares met became a piazza commonly known as the Quattro Canti di Città. Each *canto*, or canton, is the *spigolo*, or corner, or a *mandamento*, one of the four historic quarters of the city: Tribunali, Cas-tellammare, Palazzo Reale, and Monte di Pietà. A *canto*, in Palermo, is a corner.

But of course, a *canto* in Italian is also a song, or a section of an epic poem. In the pages that you have just finished read-ing, the four cantos form a fifth canto, invisible to the eye but unmistakable to all those who have left Palermo: *il canto dell'assenza*—the canto of absence.

Acknowledgments

I thank:

My father for his silences.

My mother for her words.

My sister, Gianna, for the love in her eyes when she looks at me.

My friends Fabrizio Zanca and Antonella Romano for the feelings we've shared.

I thank:

Camilla Baresani, Francesca Lancini, Alberto Cristofori, Alfredo Rapetti, Laura Ballio, Alba Donati, Alessia Algani, Roberto Andò, and Roberto Gobbi for their invaluable help; Filippo la Mantia for having taken a picture I've kept with me since 1983; Ferdinando Scianna and Marpessa Hennink for their generosity.

I thank:

Elisabetta Sgarbi for being the rockingest publisher I've ever known.

And I thank Palermo for my being born there.

GIUSEPPE DI PIAZZA began his career in journalism in 1979 with the newspaper *L'Ora*. He has worked for such Italian publications as *Sette*, where he was director, and for *Max* as editor in chief. He is currently an editorial director at *Corriere della Sera* and teaches a master's course in journalism at the IULM University of Languages and Communication in Milan. *The Four Corners of Palermo* is his first novel.

ANTONY SHUGAAR's most recent translations include Strega Prize winners *Resistance Is Futile* by Walter Siti and *Story of My People* by Edoardo Nesi, as well as *On Earth as It Is in Heaven* by Davide Enia, *Romanzo Criminale* by Giancarlo De Cataldo, and *Not All Bastards Are from Vienna* by Andrea Molesini. He is currently writing a book about translation for the University of Virginia Press.